The Spooky Story

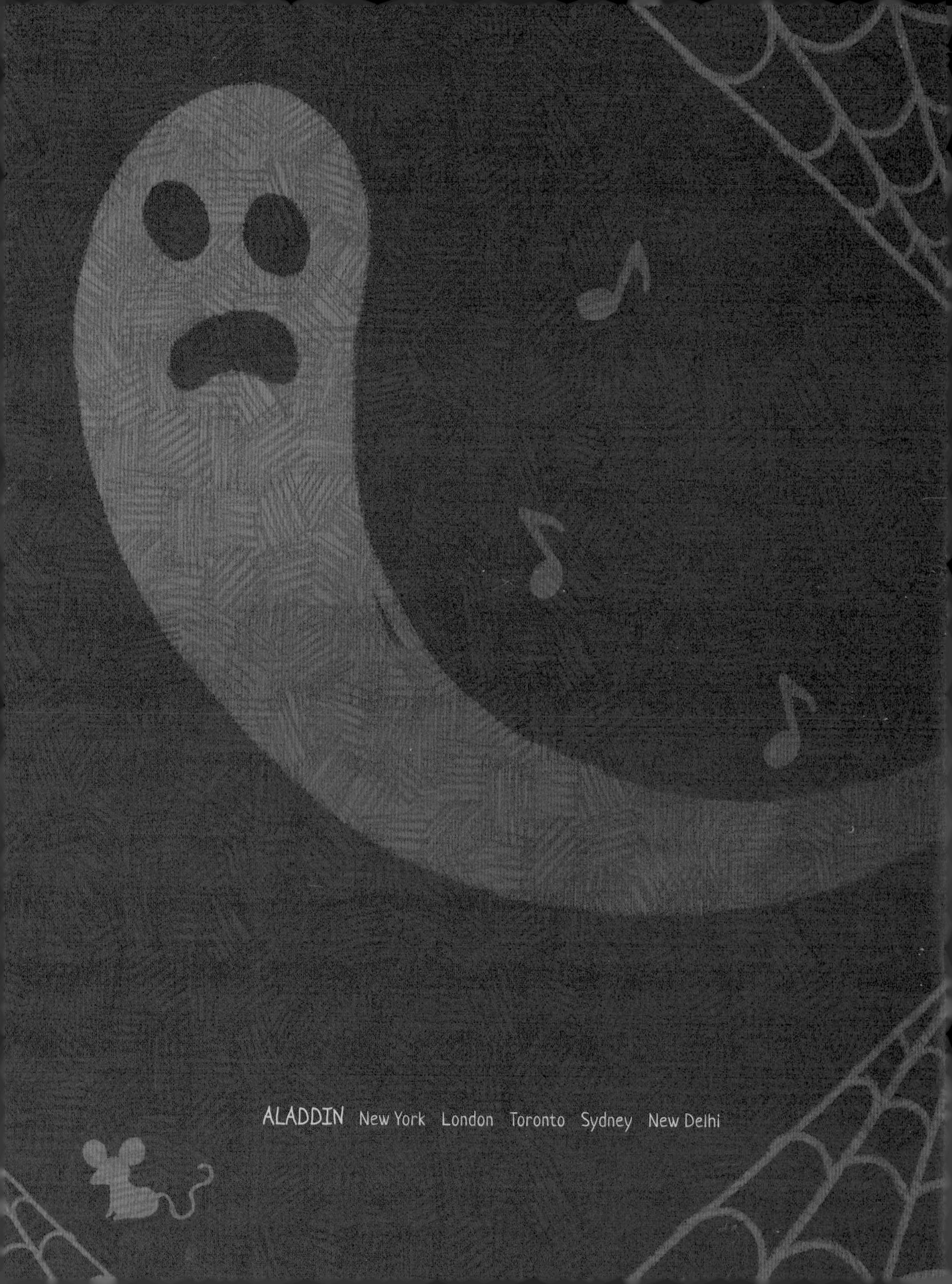

ALADDIN New York London Toronto Sydney New Delhi

Paige
PROVES IT
BOOK 2:
The Spooky Story
Facts
BY AMY MARIE STADELMANN

ALADDIN
Simon & Schuster Children's Publishing Division
1230 Avenue of the Americas, New York, New York 10020
First Aladdin edition February 2023
Text copyright © 2023 by Amy Marie Stadelmann
Illustrations copyright © 2023 by Amy Marie Stadelmann
All rights reserved, including the right of reproduction in whole or in part in any form.
ALADDIN and related logo are registered trademarks of Simon & Schuster, Inc.
For information about special discounts for bulk purchases, please contact Simon & Schuster Special Sales at 1-866-506-1949 or business@simonandschuster.com.
The Simon & Schuster Speakers Bureau can bring authors to your live event. For more information or to book an event contact the Simon & Schuster Speakers Bureau at 1-866-248-3049 or visit our website at www.simonspeakers.com.
Book designed by Tiara Iandiorio
The illustrations for this book were rendered in pencil and digitally colored.
The text of this book was set in Austral Slab.
Manufactured in China 1022 SCP
10 9 8 7 6 5 4 3 2 1
Library of Congress Catalog Number 2022943253
ISBN 978-1-5344-5164-3 (hc)
ISBN 978-1-5344-5163-6 (pbk)
ISBN 978-1-5344-5165-0 (ebook)

For story lovers,
both fact and fiction!

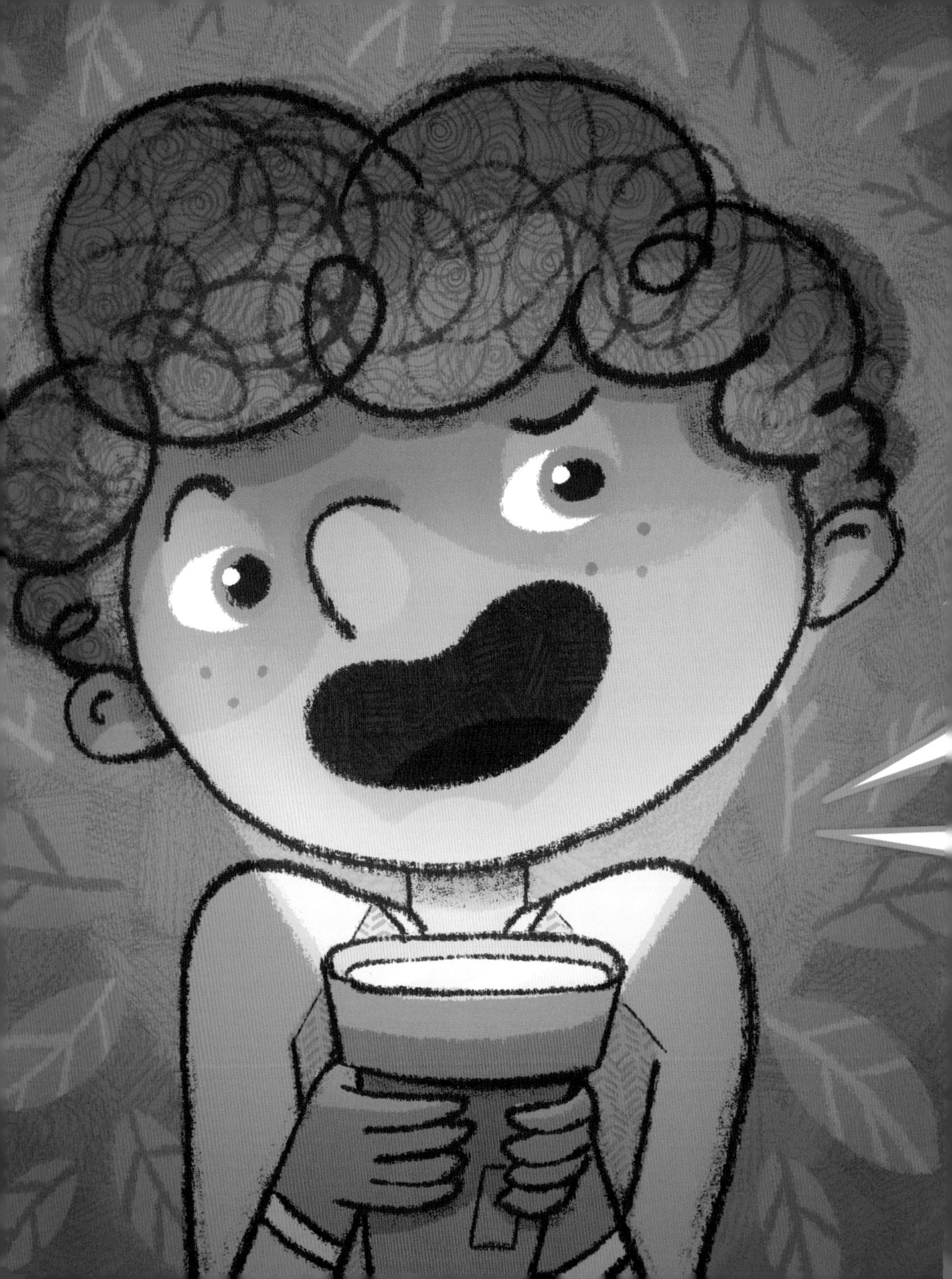

Chapter One

BEWARE!

This spooky story is **scary** and totally **true!**

Everyone knows that the
Evergreen Street Music School
is **haunted!**

Invisible voices sing scary songs in the hallways!

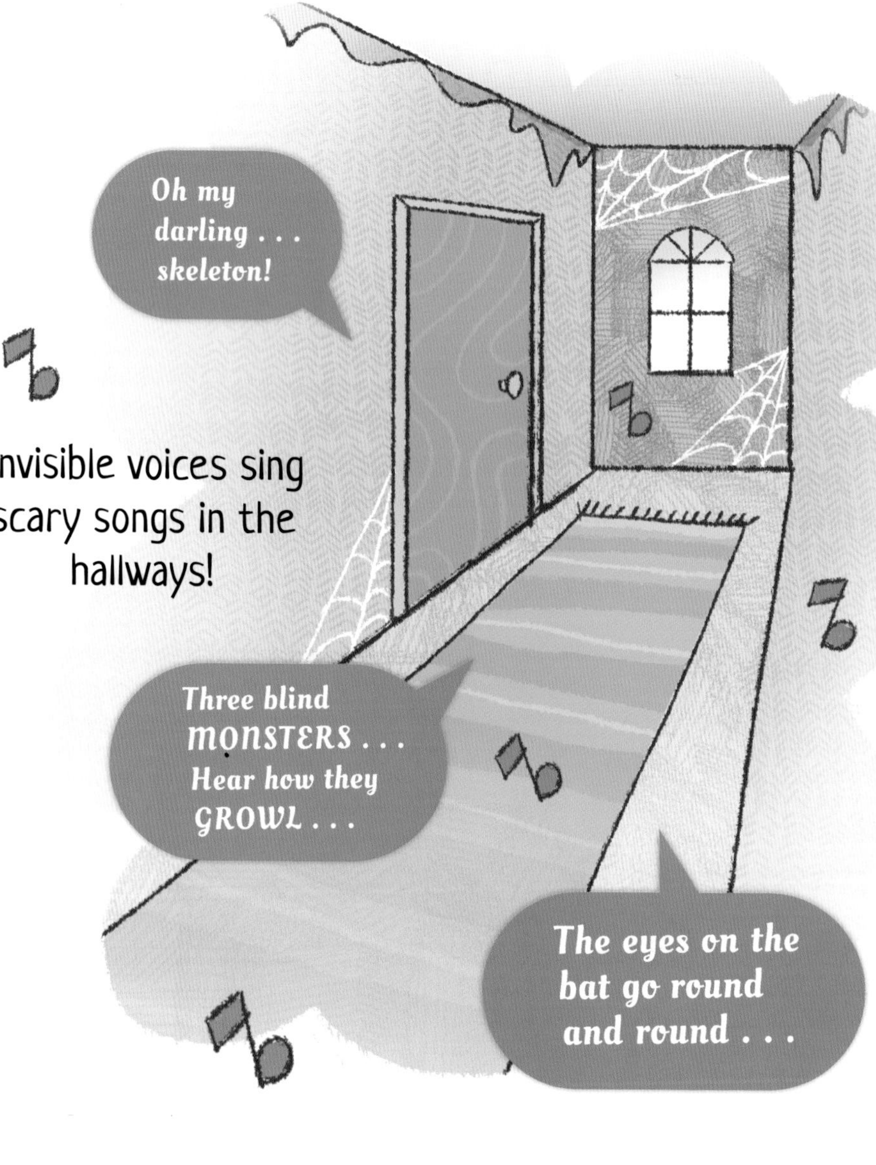
Oh my darling . . . skeleton!
Three blind MONSTERS . . . Hear how they GROWL . . .
The eyes on the bat go round and round . . .

Ghosts are seen tap-dancing on the stairs!

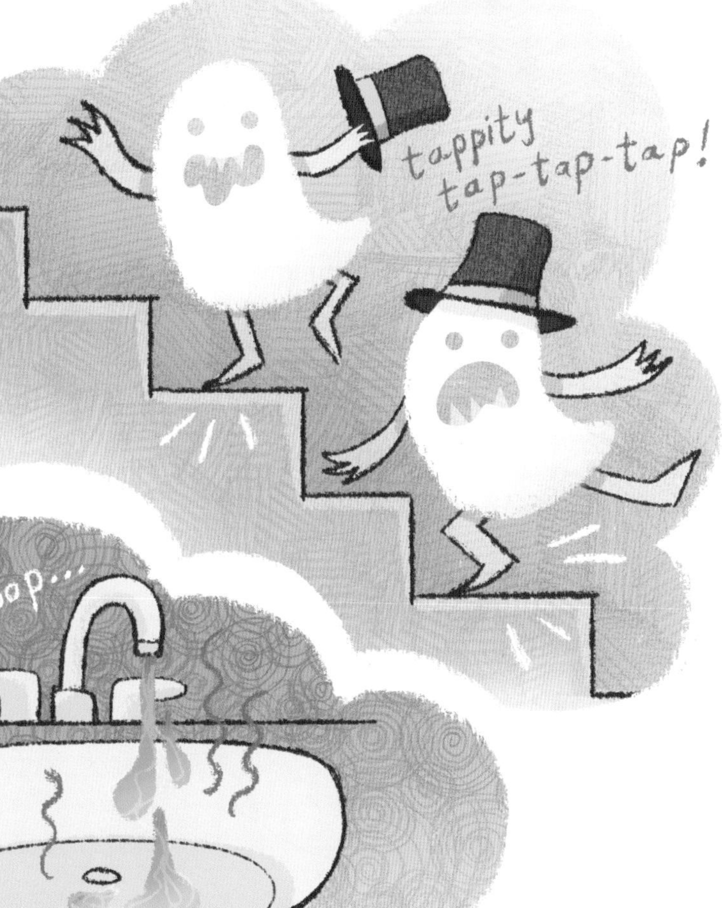
tappity
tap-tap-tap!

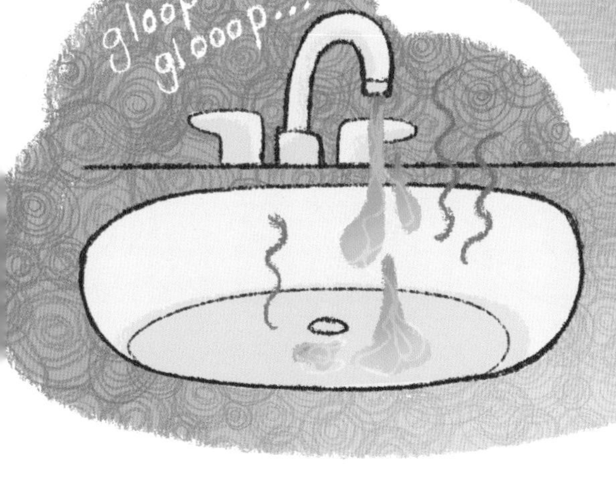
gloop
glooop...

And BOOGERS
even ooze from the
bathroom sink—

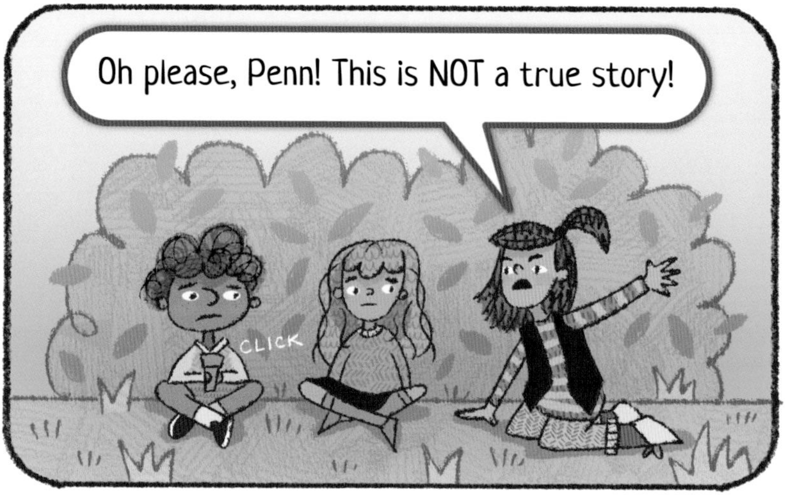
Oh please, Penn! This is NOT a true story!
CLICK

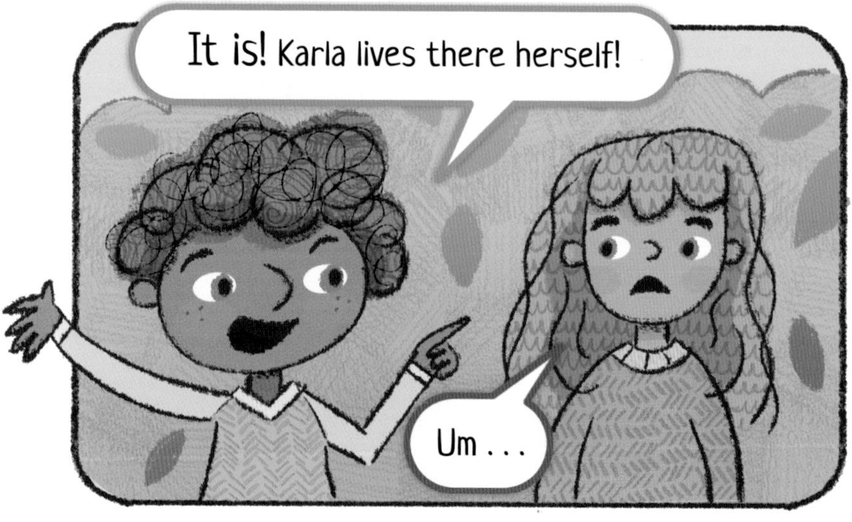
It is! Karla lives there herself!
Um . . .

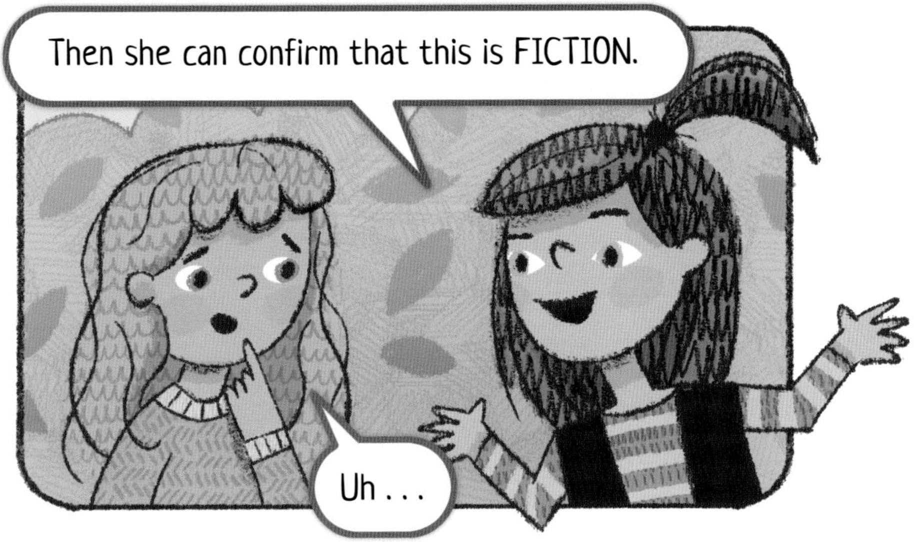
Then she can confirm that this is FICTION.
Uh . . .

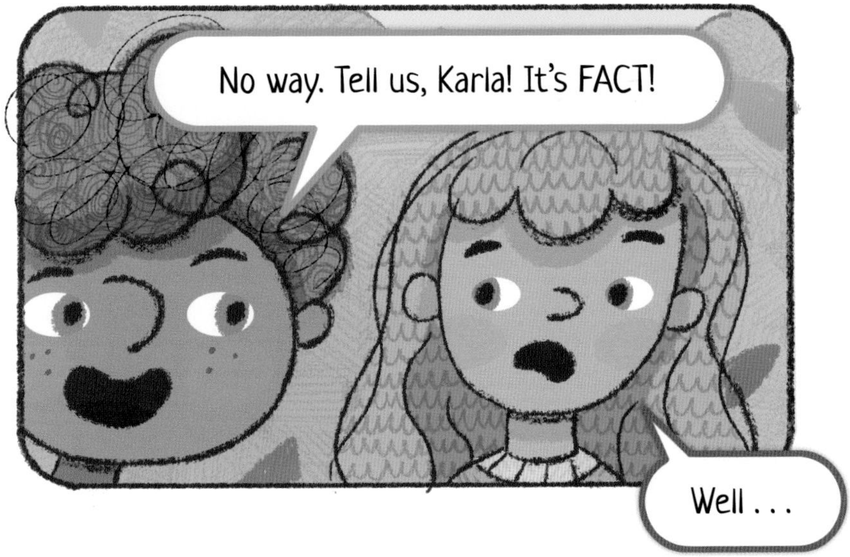
No way. Tell us, Karla! It's FACT!
Well . . .

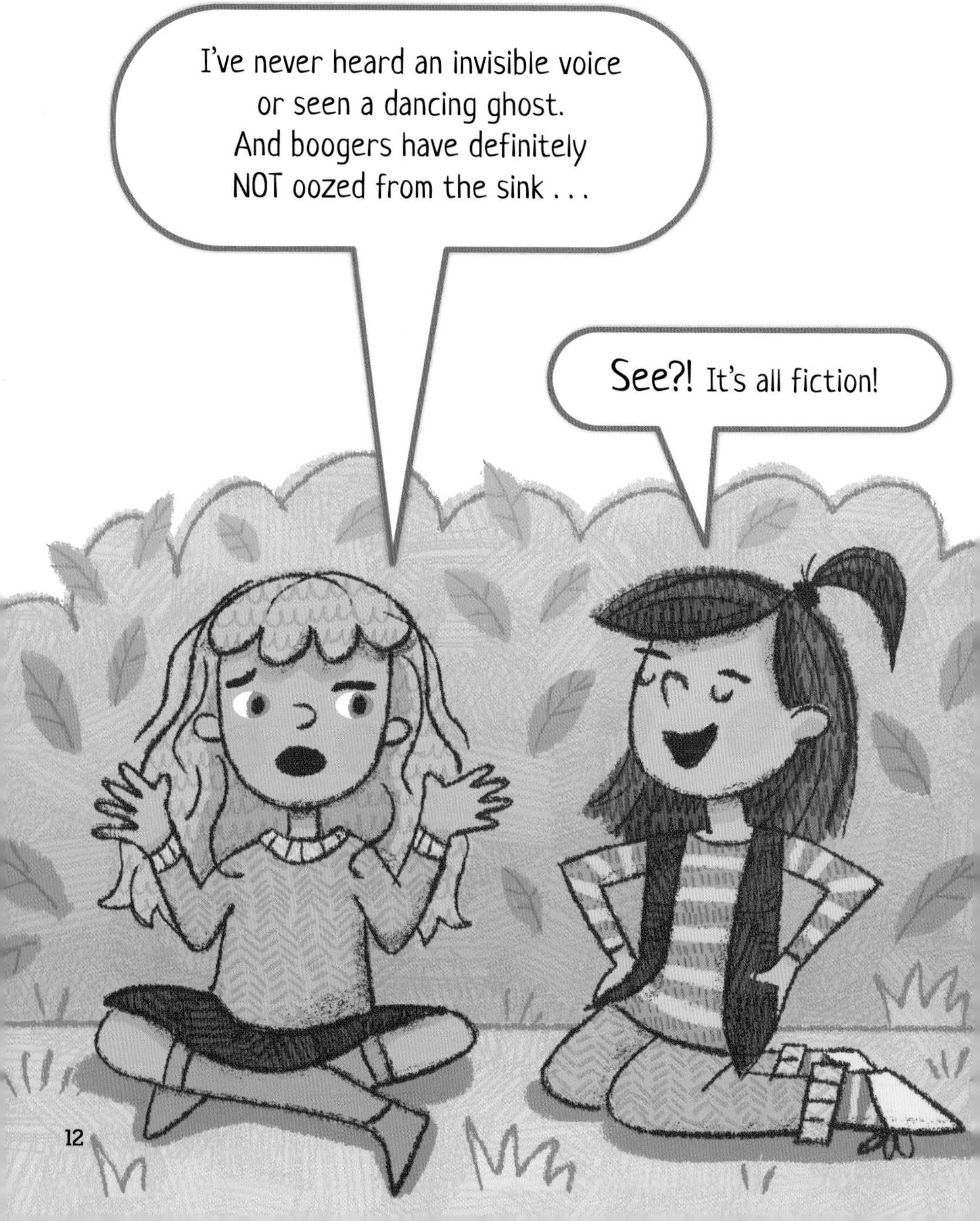
I've never heard an invisible voice or seen a dancing ghost. And boogers have definitely NOT oozed from the sink . . .
See?! It's all fiction!

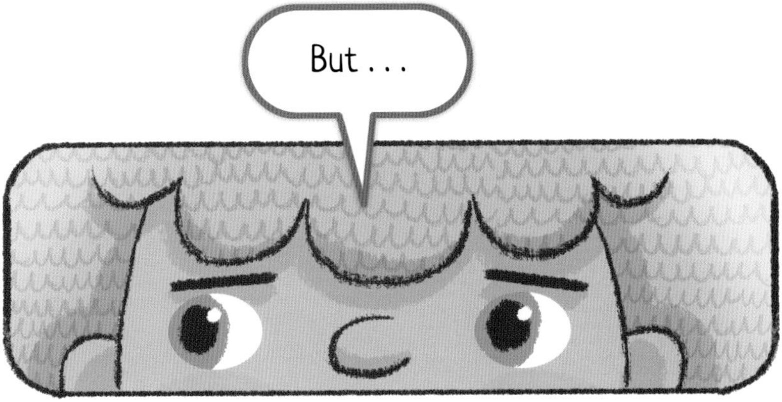
But . . .

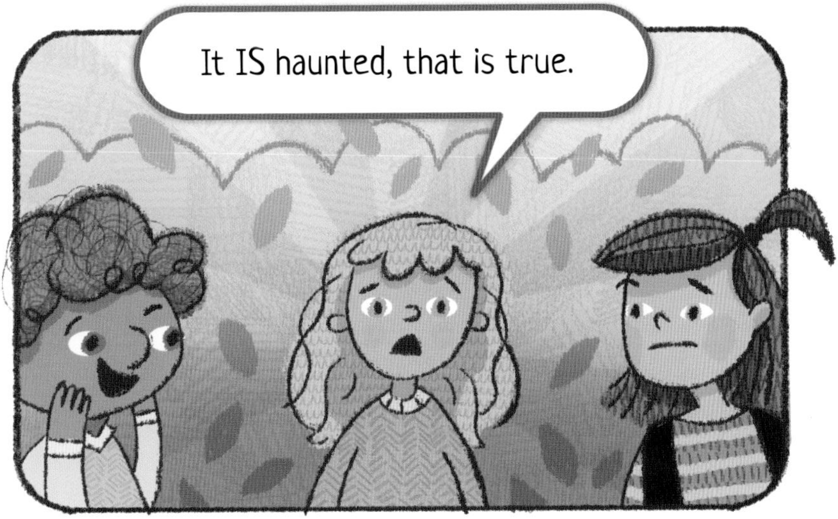
It IS haunted, that is true.

Well, that took a turn.

Allow me to introduce myself. I'm a Fact Collector.

My name is Paige.

I love facts.

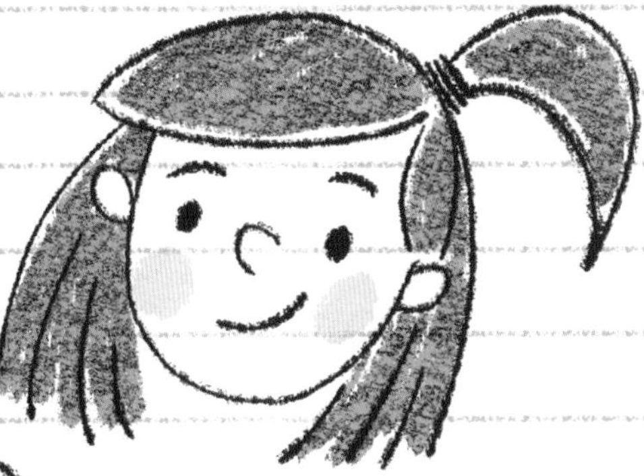

I love learning facts,

collecting facts,

and proving facts.

You could say that
I'm fact-obsessed!

Facts are true pieces of information.

I collect lots of amazing facts in my Fact Diary.

A group of zebras is called a dazzle.

The ancient Egyptians invented toothpaste.

If it's not in my diary, then it's not a fact! It's fiction.

You see, there are two kinds of stories.

Fiction and nonfiction.

Fiction is all imagined and made-up.

Nonfiction is all facts and truth.

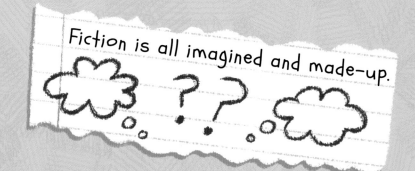

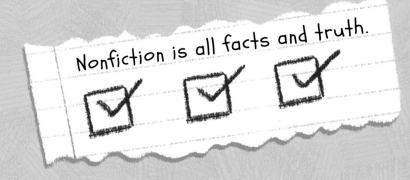

Obviously, I prefer nonfiction.

Facts only, please!

But ghost stories are fiction, right?

Unless . . .

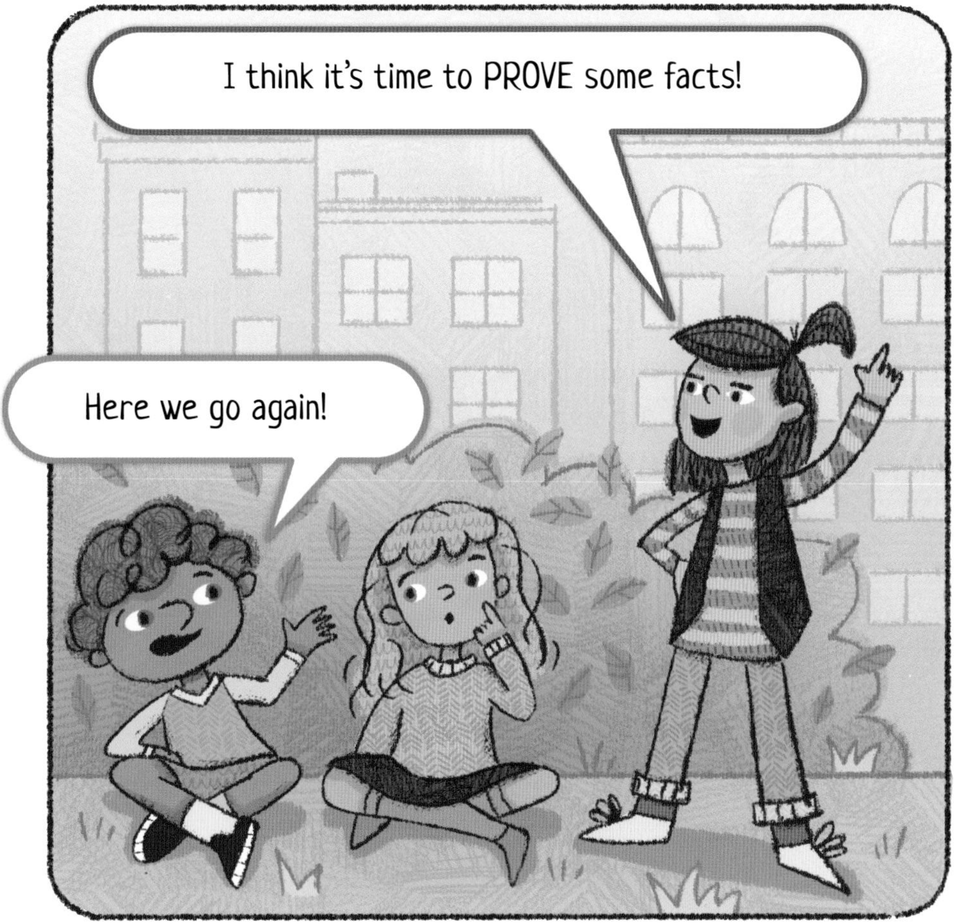
I think it's time to PROVE some facts!
Here we go again!

Chapter Two

First things first. Here are the facts about the Evergreen Street Music School.

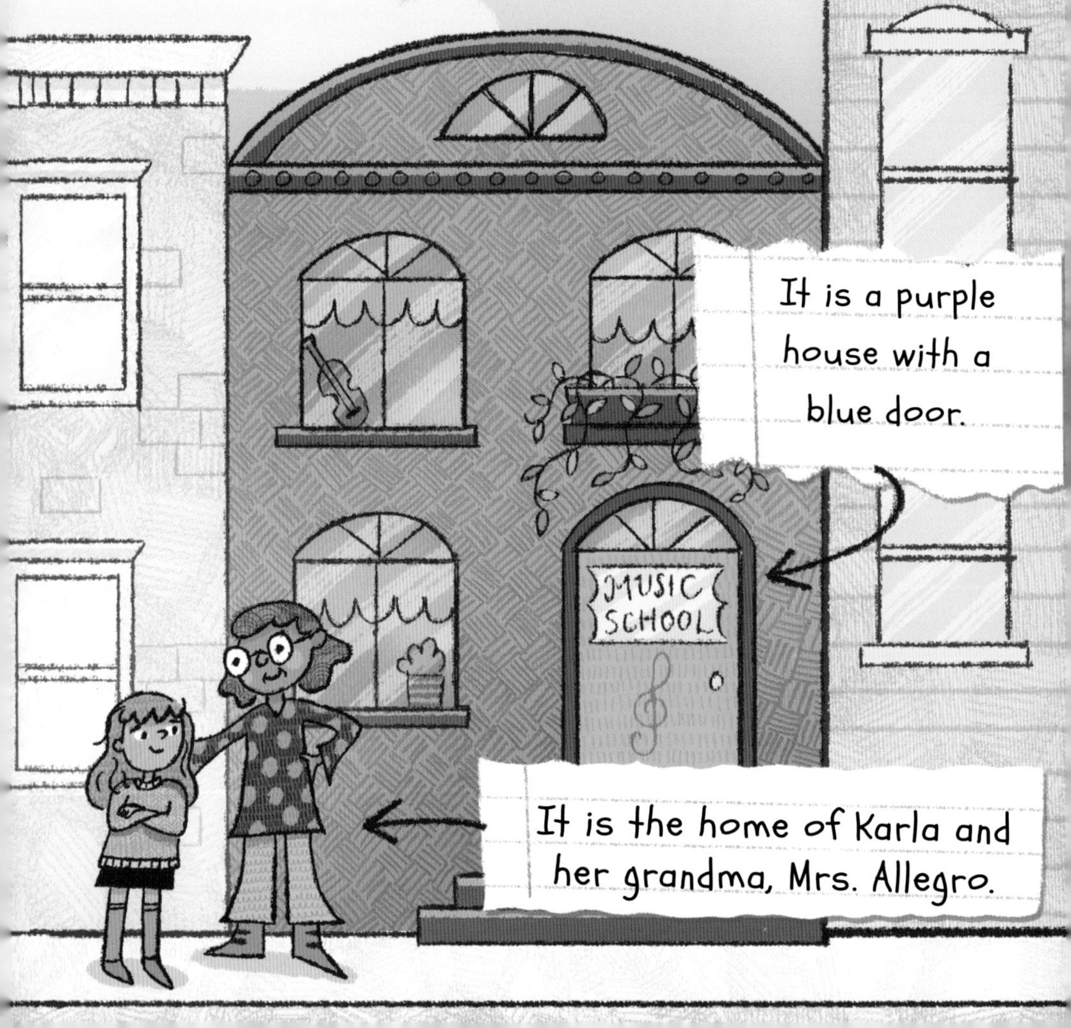
It is a purple house with a blue door.
MUSIC SCHOOL
It is the home of Karla and her grandma, Mrs. Allegro.

Karla and Mrs. Allegro live upstairs.

The school is downstairs, where
Mrs. Allegro teaches all the music classes.

It's also a fact that many neighbors take music classes there.

Here's what they say:

Wonderful classes! My harp playing has never sounded so spooky.

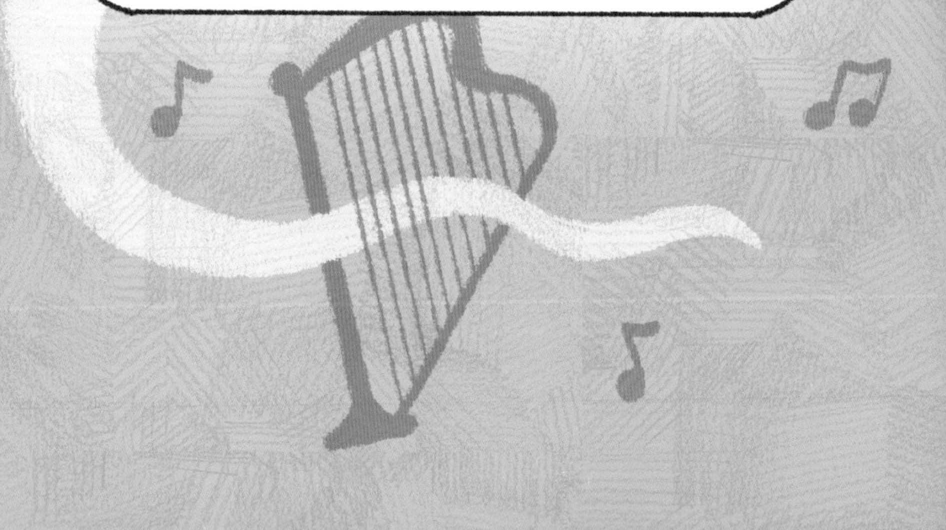

Ms. M

"⭐⭐⭐⭐☆"

Helped me perfect my birdcalls. Needs less kids and ghosts!

Mr. Drufus

Rockin' music school! Totally haunted, though.

Kid with a pet rock

But just because someone says something doesn't make it a fact.

A fact is proven when there is evidence. Without it, it's a guess.

Here's an example.

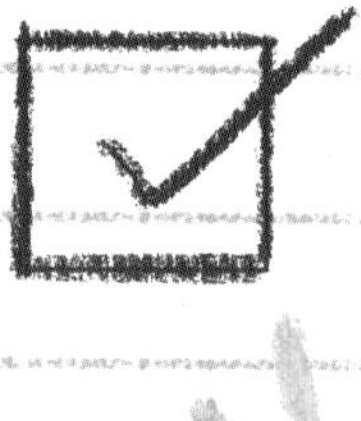

Fact: Chameleons are lizards who have the ability to change their skin color.

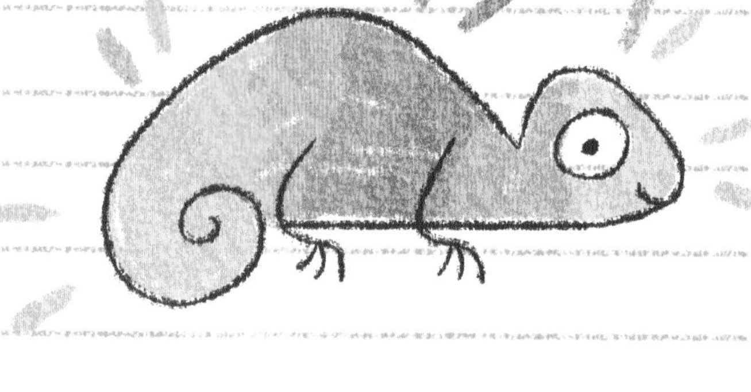

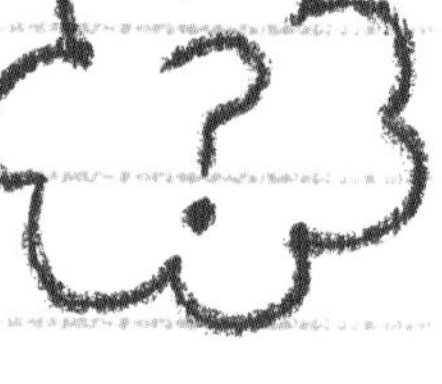

Scientists guessed they changed color to hide from danger.

But after collecting and studying evidence,
this guess was proven NOT to be a fact!

☑ Fact: Chameleons change color
based on temperature and mood.

So, in order to prove whether a story is fiction or fact, we need evidence. Everyone might SAY the music school is haunted, but Karla actually lives there.

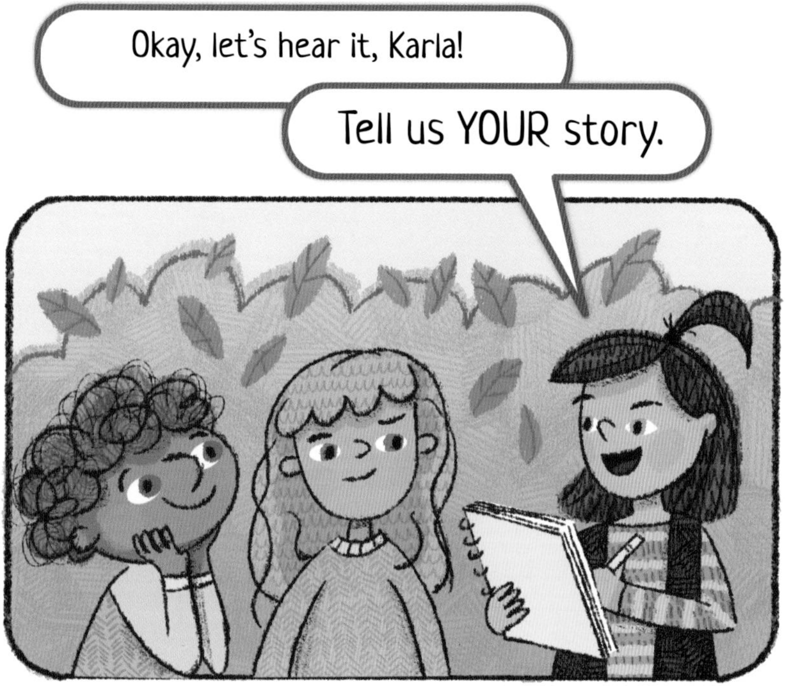
Okay, let's hear it, Karla!
Tell us YOUR story.

And since I am a very good Fact Collector, I take notes while Karla talks. Now I have an ACTUAL list to investigate, instead of Penn's fiction.

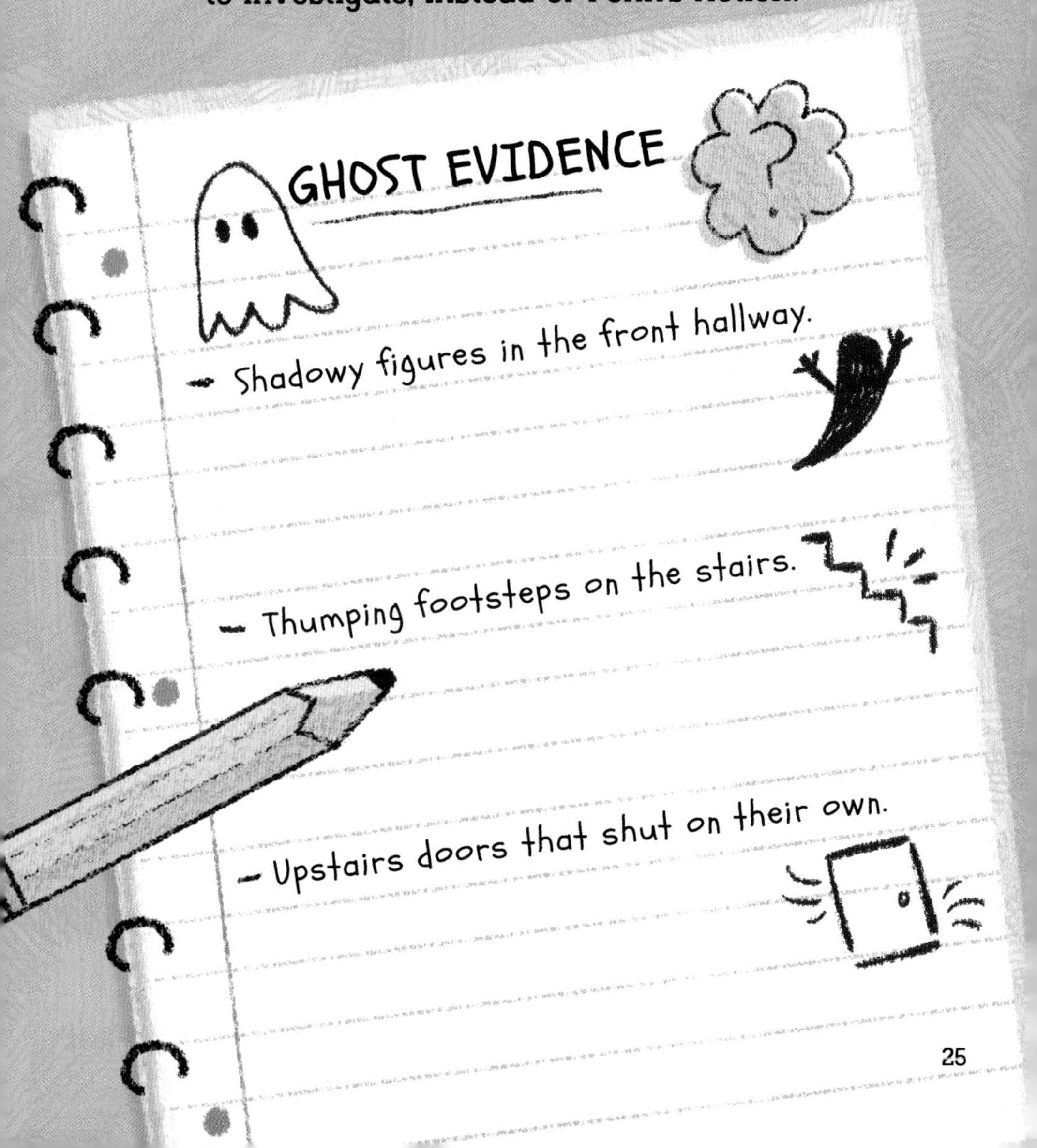
GHOST EVIDENCE
- Shadowy figures in the front hallway.
- Thumping footsteps on the stairs.
- Upstairs doors that shut on their own.

Chapter Three

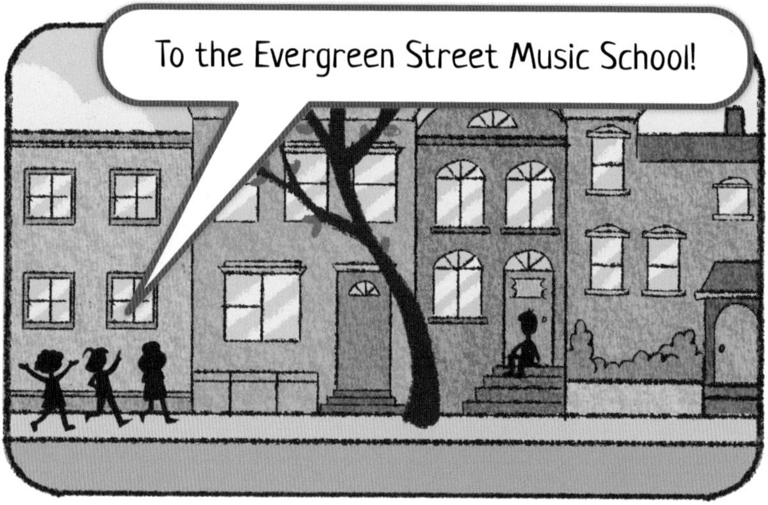
To the Evergreen Street Music School!

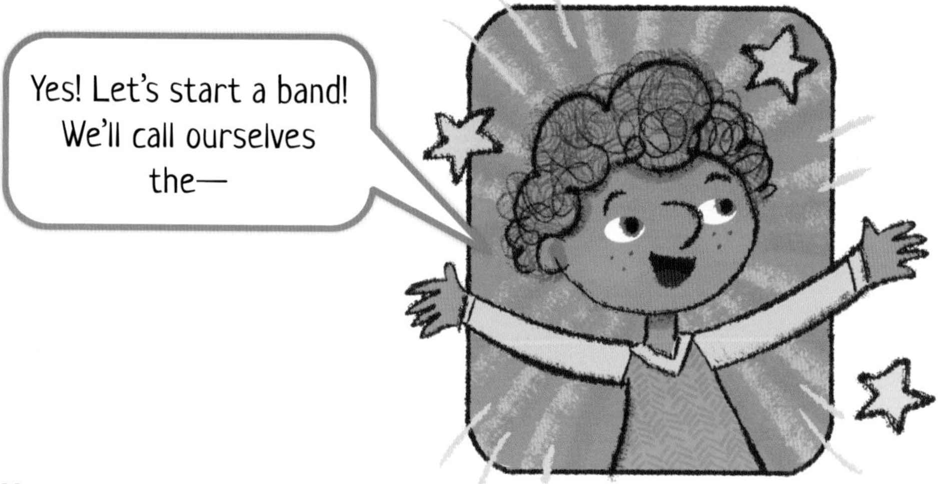
Yes! Let's start a band! We'll call ourselves the—

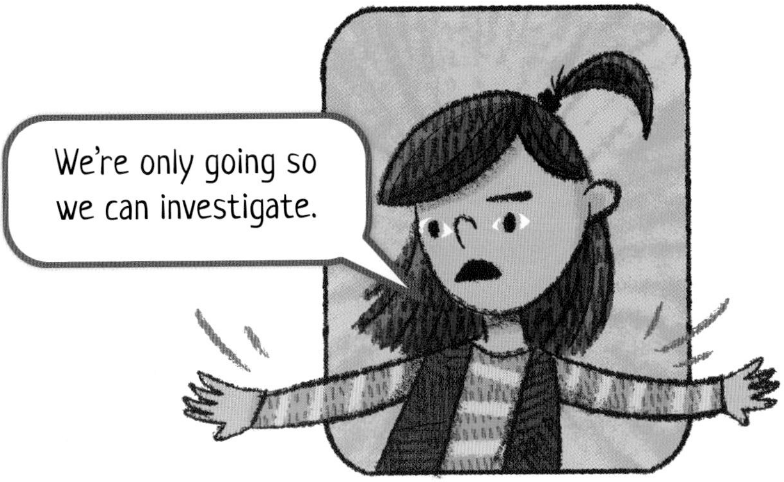
We're only going so
we can investigate.

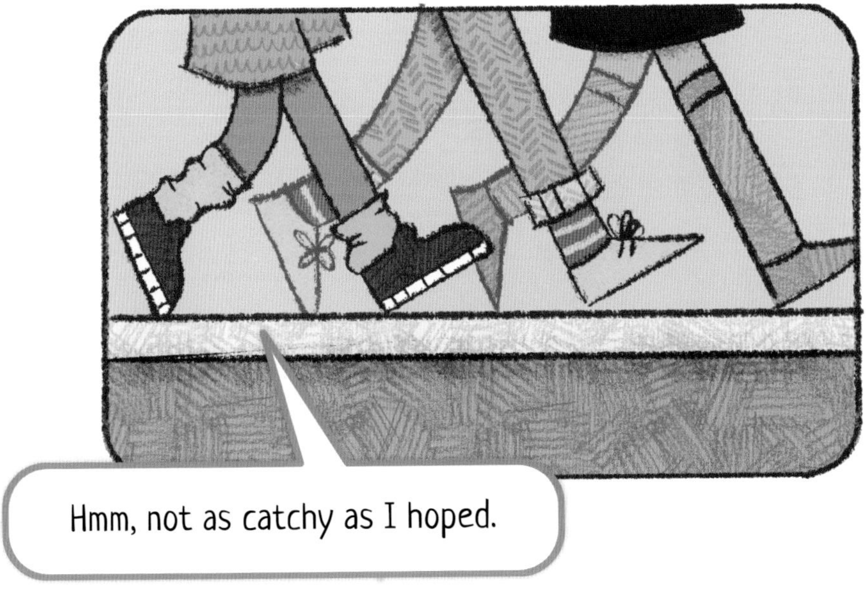
Hmm, not as catchy as I hoped.

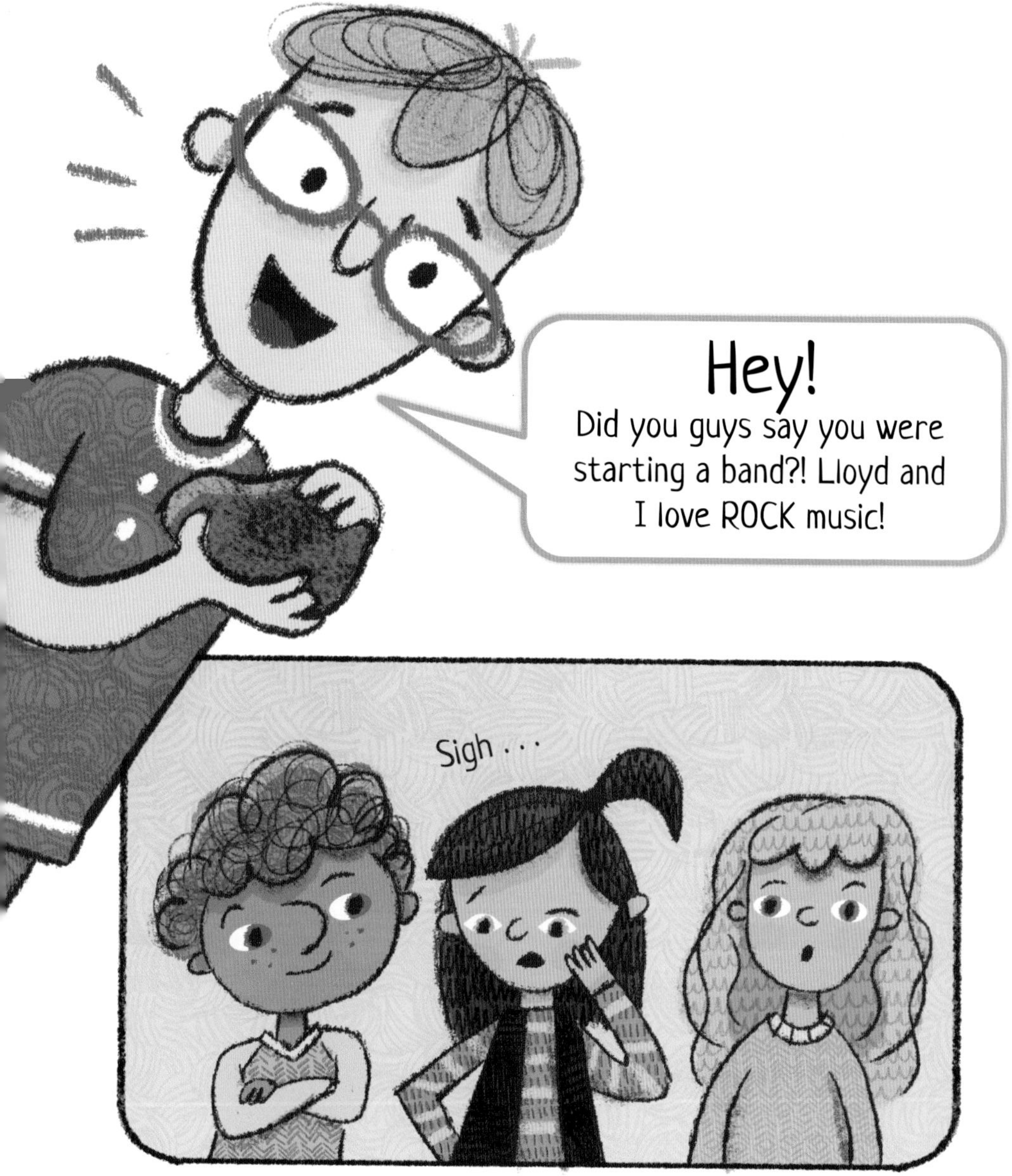
Hey!
Did you guys say you were starting a band?! Lloyd and I love ROCK music!
Sigh . . .

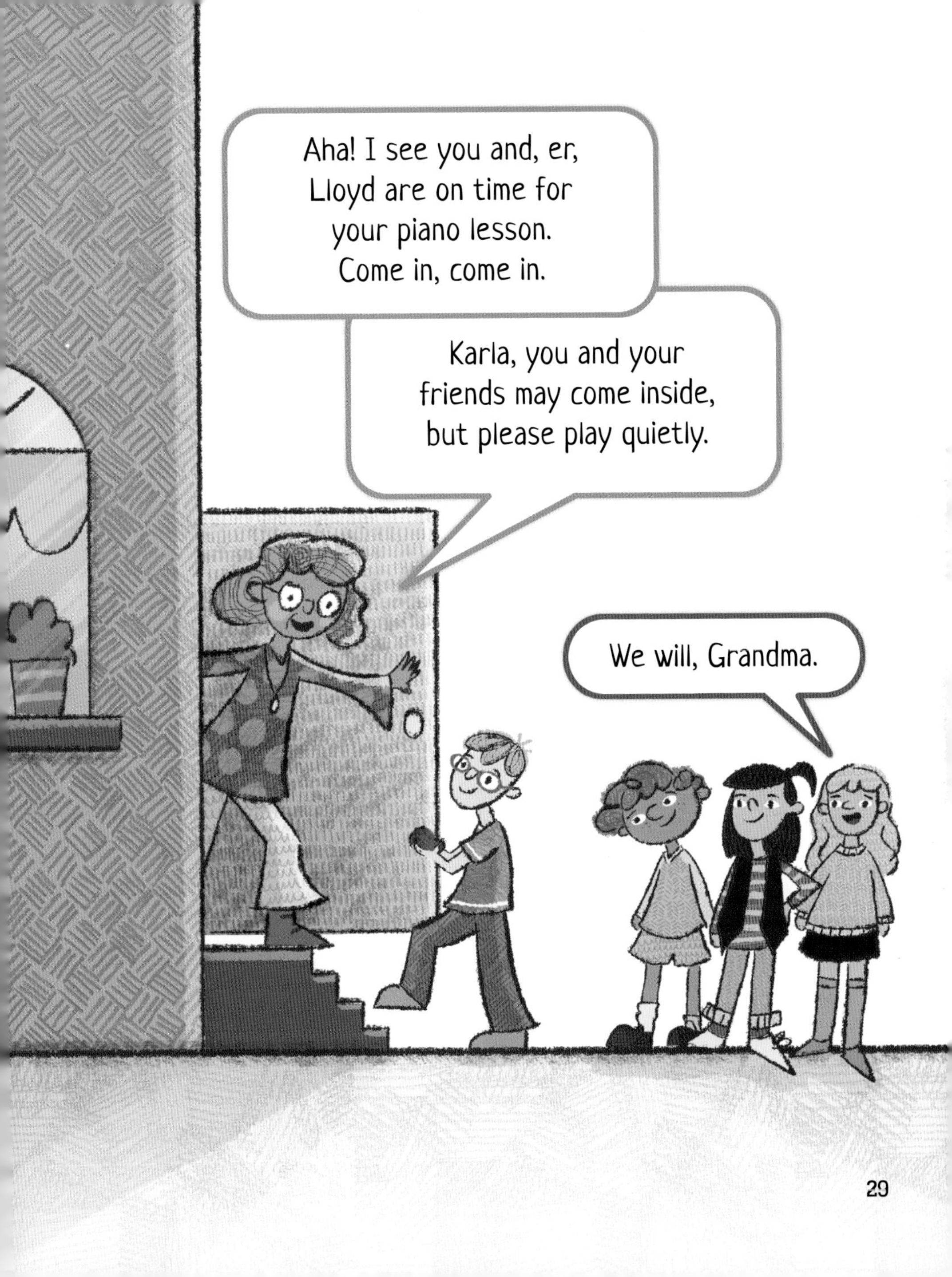
Aha! I see you and, er, Lloyd are on time for your piano lesson. Come in, come in.
Karla, you and your friends may come inside, but please play quietly.
We will, Grandma.

We're in!

Now it's time to explore.

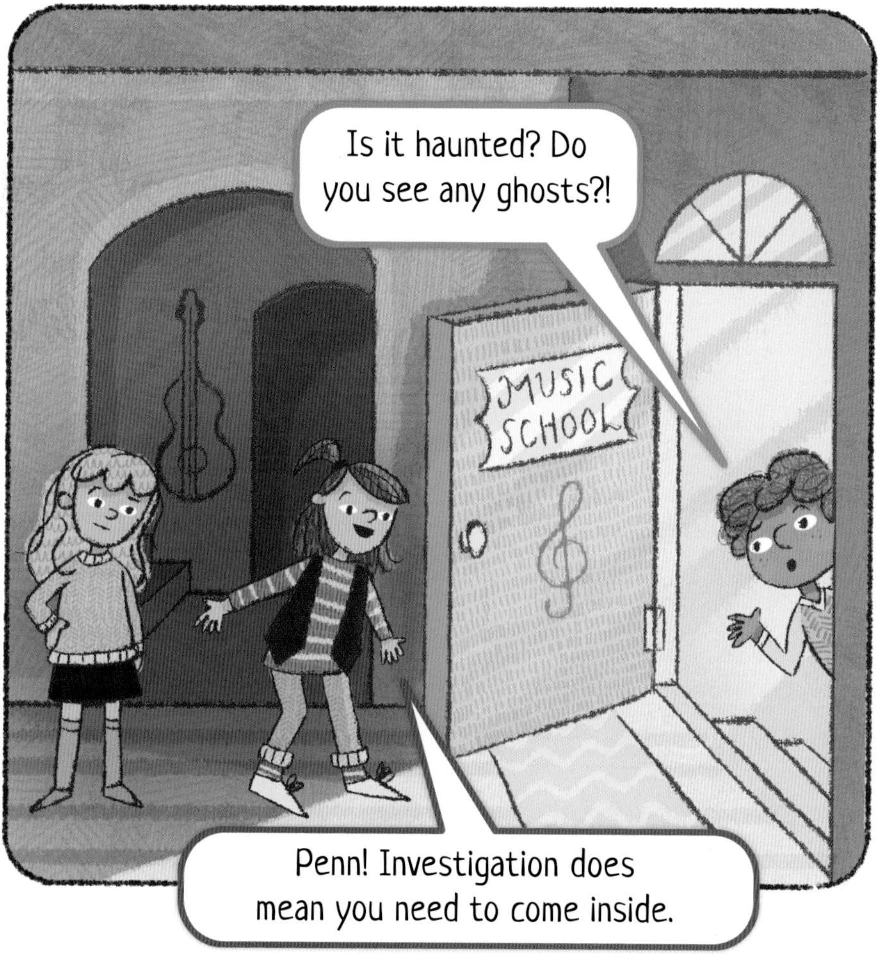
Is it haunted? Do you see any ghosts?!
MUSIC SCHOOL
Penn! Investigation does mean you need to come inside.

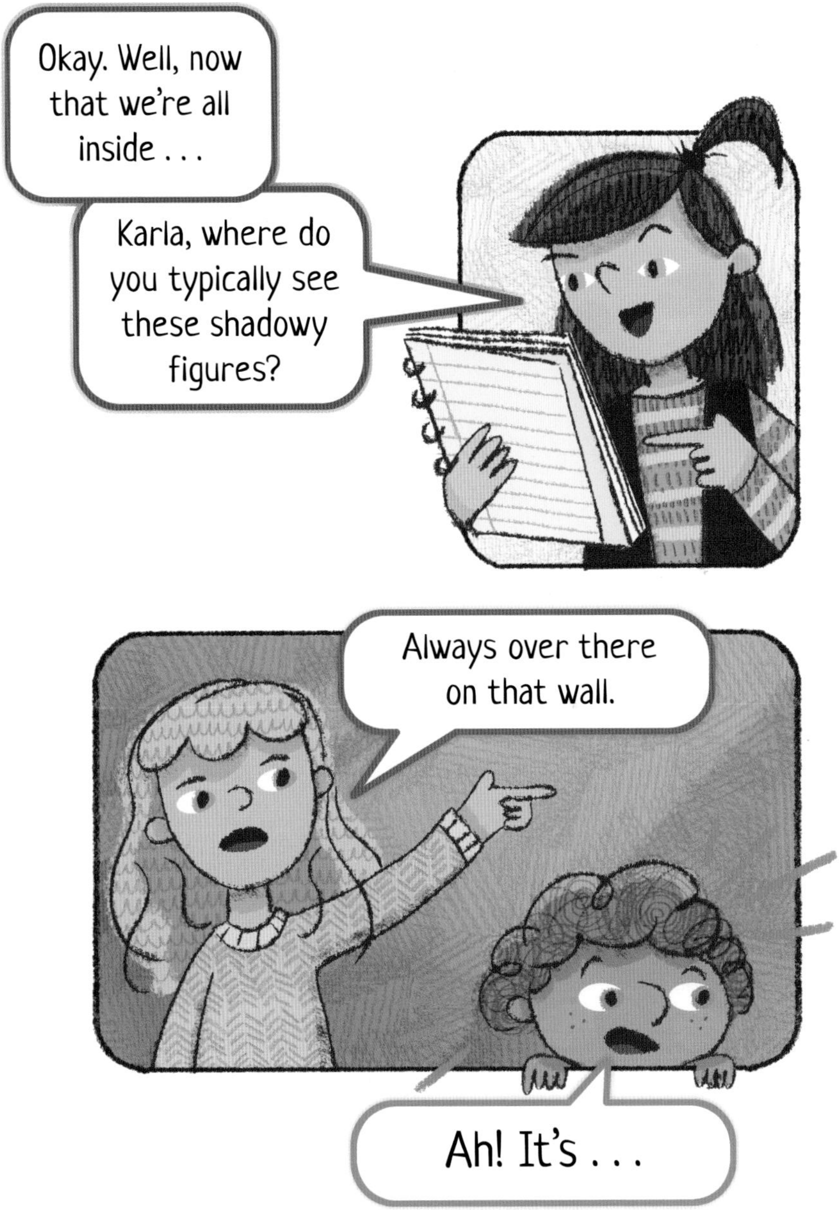
Okay. Well, now that we're all inside . . .
Karla, where do you typically see these shadowy figures?
Always over there on that wall.
Ah! It's . . .

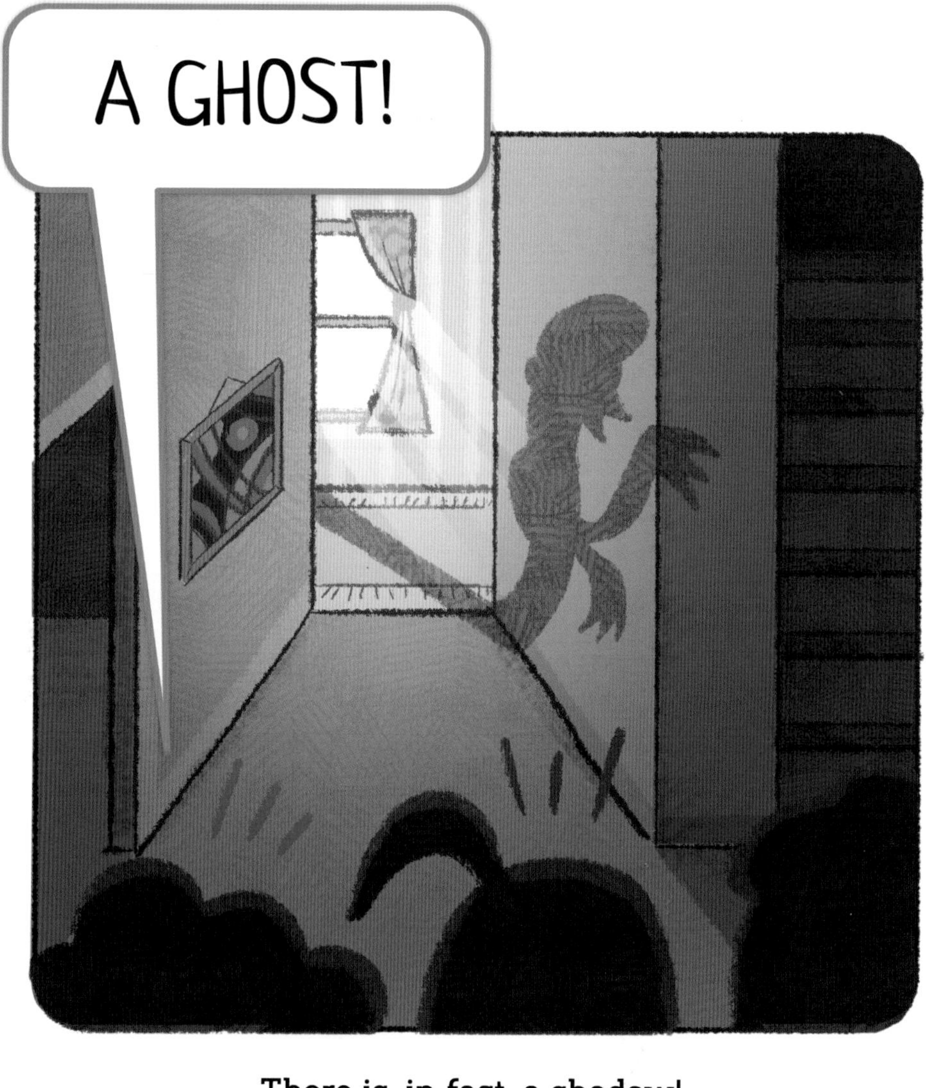
A GHOST!

There is, in fact, a shadow!

But is it a ghost?

A good place to begin with facts is observations.
These are things you can see, hear, touch,
smell, and even taste.

I write down my observations.

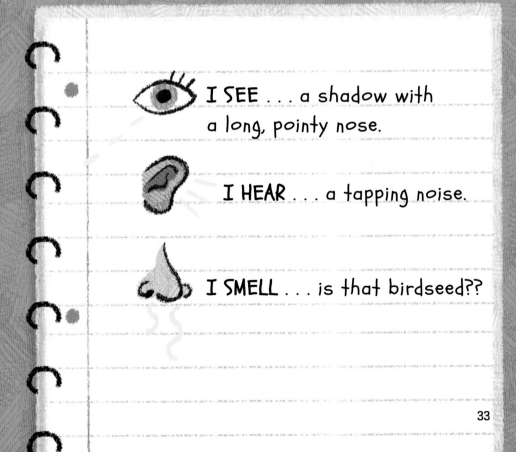

I SEE . . . a shadow with a long, pointy nose.

I HEAR . . . a tapping noise.

I SMELL . . . is that birdseed??

Also, here's the thing about shadows.
They always have a source.

shadow
source

If we look where the light is coming from,
we should find the source of the shadow.

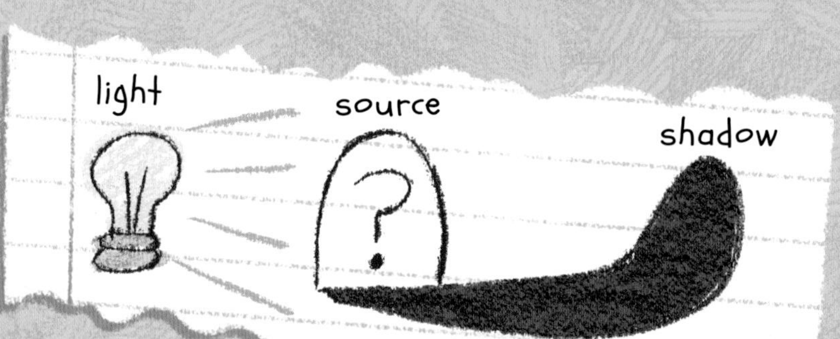
light
source
shadow

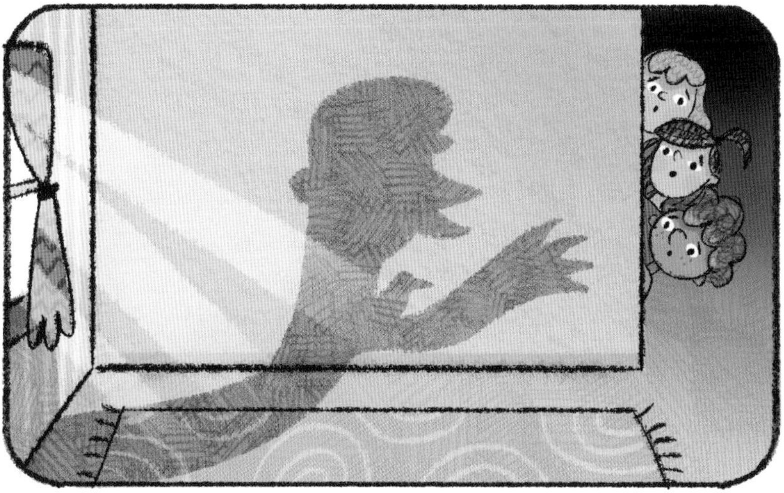

The window!

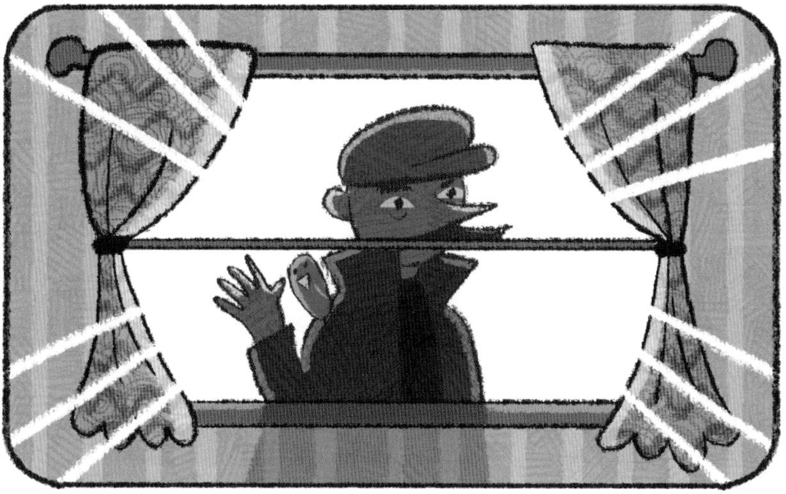

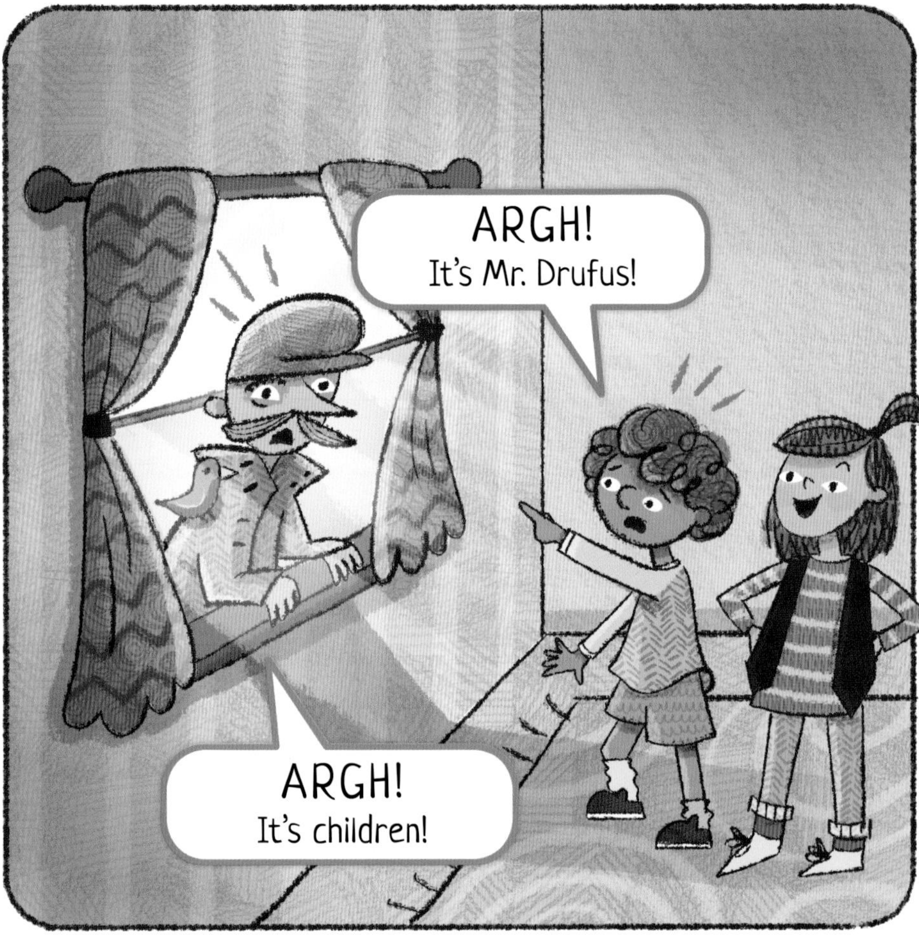
ARGH!
It's Mr. Drufus!
ARGH!
It's children!

YES! The shadows are caused by neighbors walking by! I am one step closer to proving this haunting is nothing but fic—

EXCUSE ME?

I'm actually here to deliver some very important news!

Important news?! I must take notes!

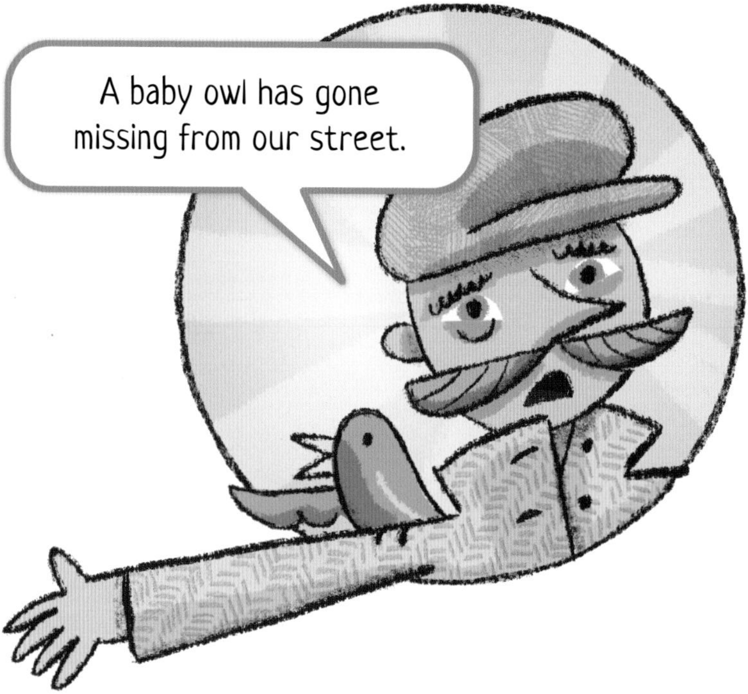
A baby owl has gone missing from our street.

Oh dear, I'm afraid I can only
investigate one thing at a time.
But, note to self, where do baby owls hide?

GHOST EVIDENCE

~~Shadowy figures in the front hallway.~~

☑ Neighbor in window.

‒ Thumping footsteps on the stairs.

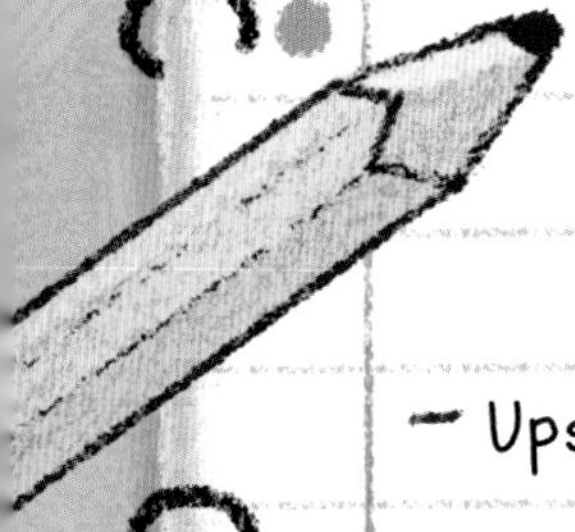

‒ Upstairs doors that shut on their own.

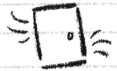

Baby owl?

Chapter Four

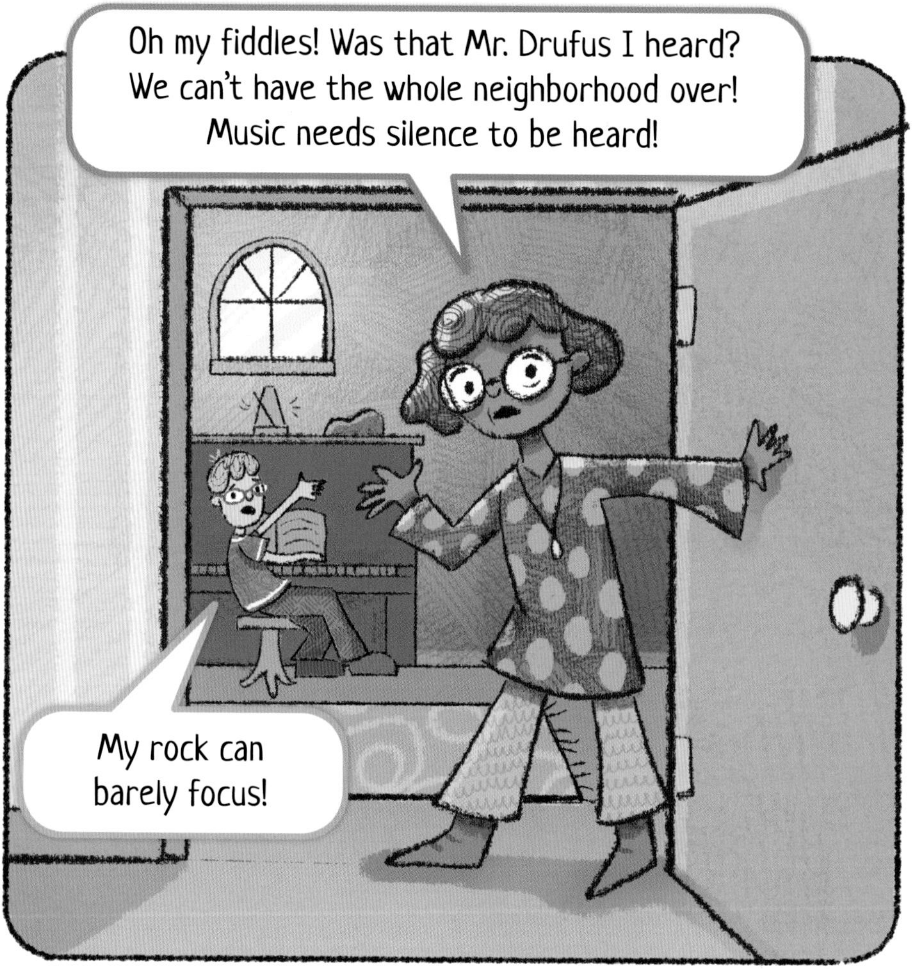
Oh my fiddles! Was that Mr. Drufus I heard? We can't have the whole neighborhood over! Music needs silence to be heard!
My rock can barely focus!

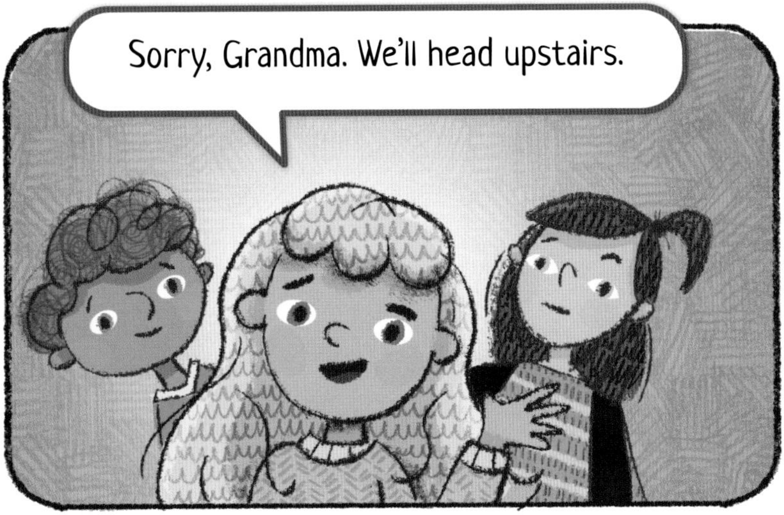
Sorry, Grandma. We'll head upstairs.

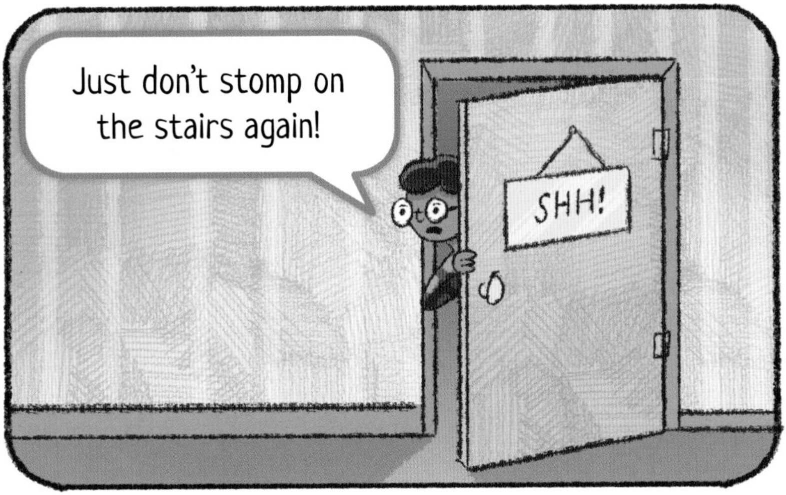
Just don't stomp on the stairs again!
SHH!

Wait . . .

"Again"?!

We haven't stomped on the stairs AT ALL.
Is Karla's grandmother hearing a ghost?!

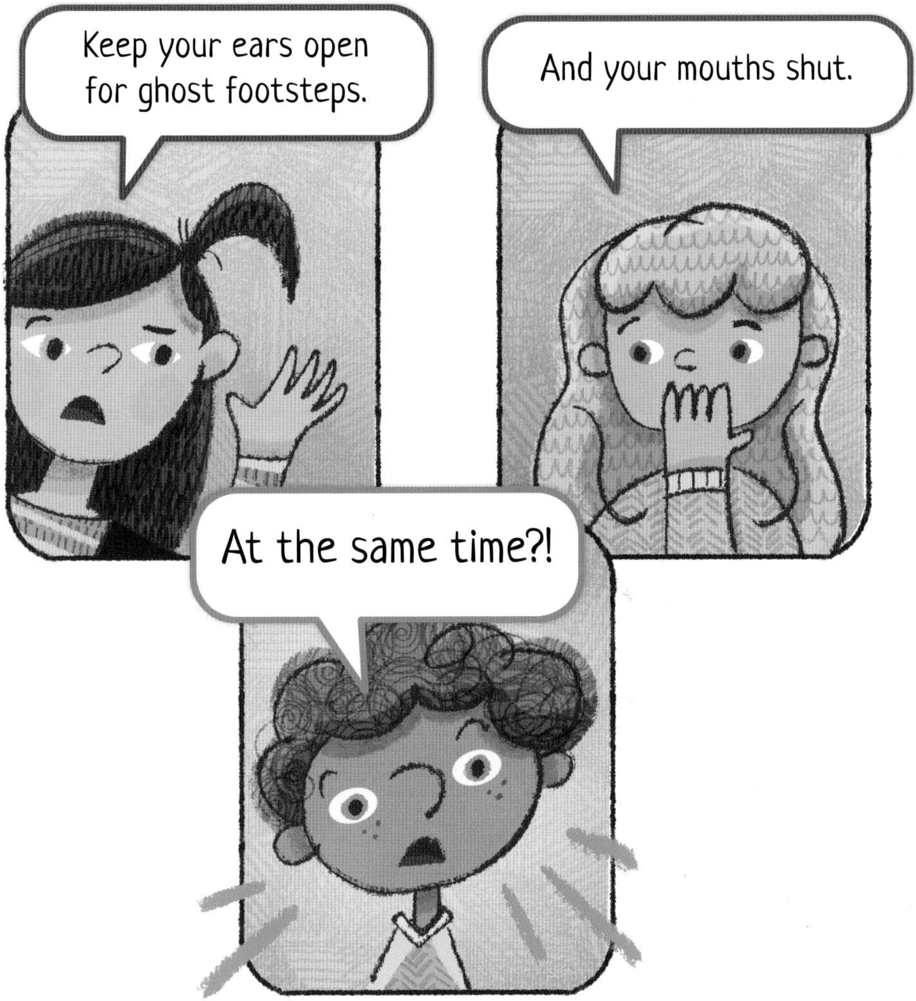
Keep your ears open for ghost footsteps.
And your mouths shut.
At the same time?!

I hear the sounds of the piano.

I hear the sound of the ceiling fan.

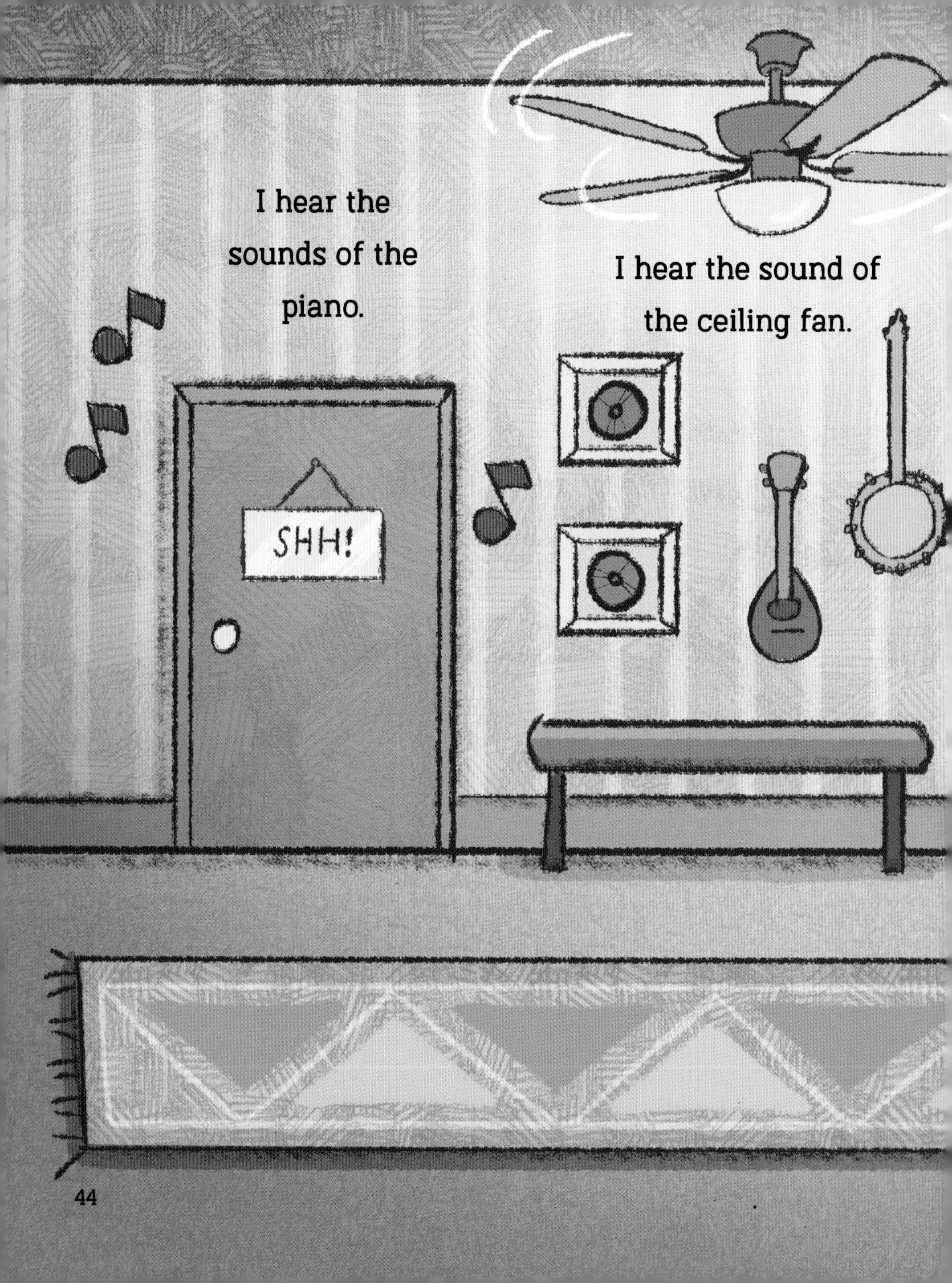
SHH!

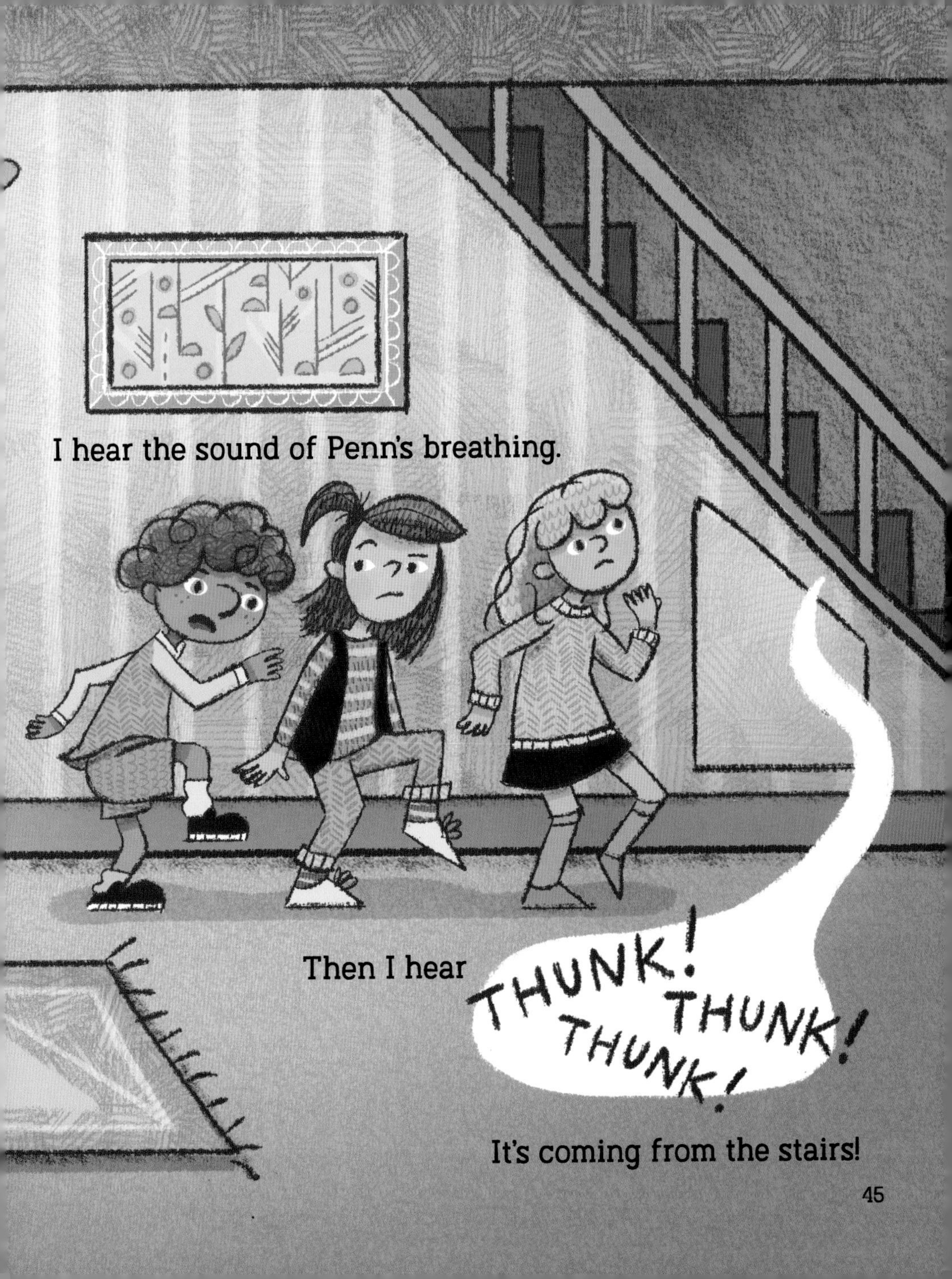
THUNK!
THUNK!
THUNK!

I hear the sound of Penn's breathing.

Then I hear

THUNK! THUNK! THUNK!

It's coming from the stairs!

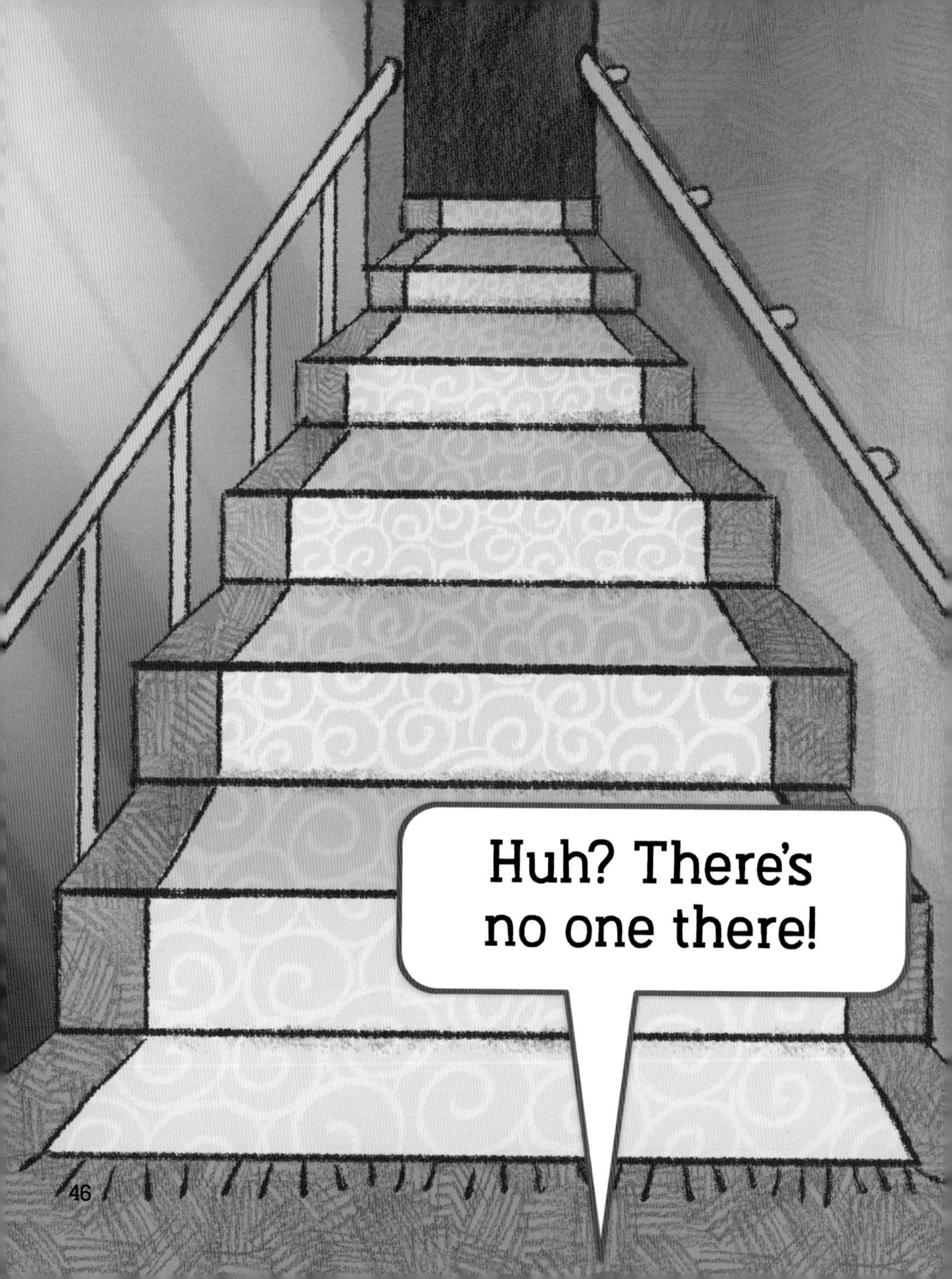
Huh? There's no one there!

So I write down my observations.

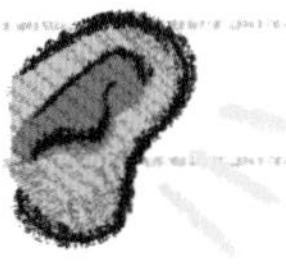

I HEAR . . . thunk, thunk, thunk.

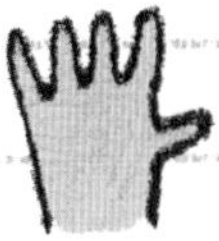

I FEEL . . . a noise vibration on the floor.

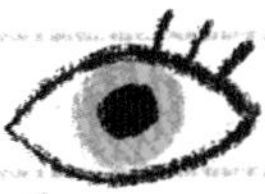

I SEE . . . nobody and nothing on the stairs!

If the noise isn't coming from ON the stairs, could it be coming from UNDER them?

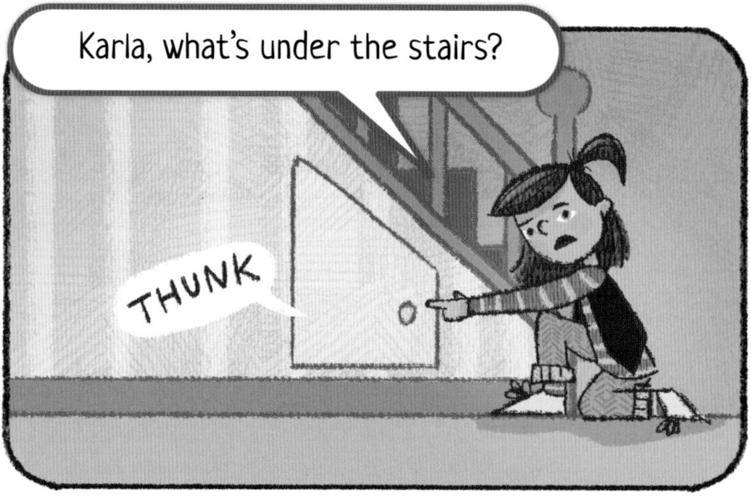
Karla, what's under the stairs?
THUNK

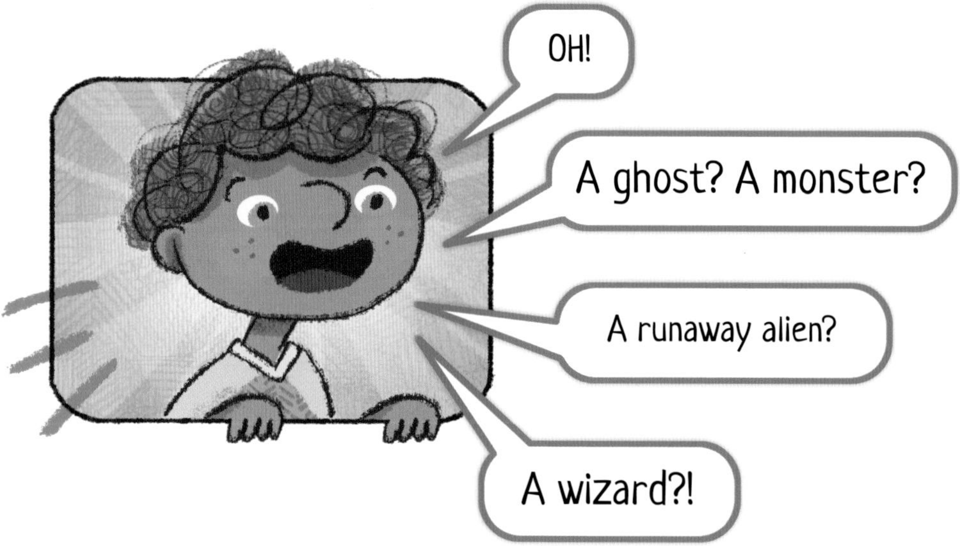
OH!
A ghost? A monster?
A runaway alien?
A wizard?!

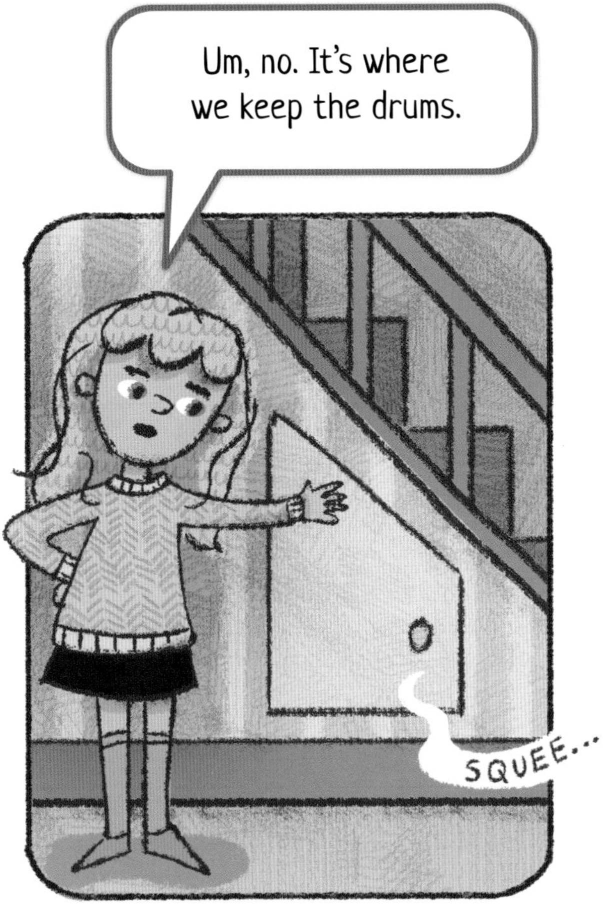
Um, no. It's where
we keep the drums.
SQUEE...

Drums can go thunk, thunk, thunk . . .
but only if someone is playing them, right?

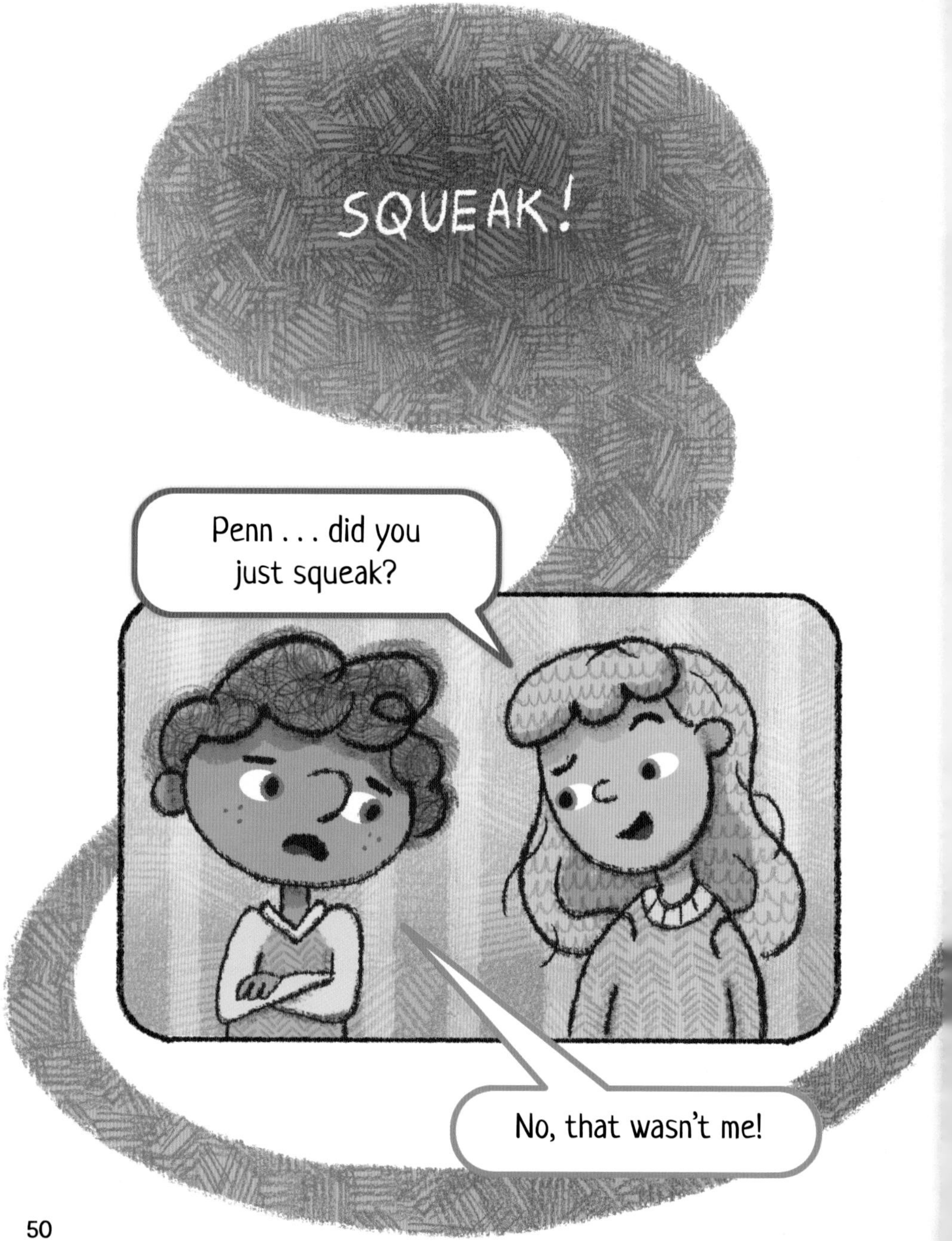
SQUEAK!
Penn . . . did you just squeak?
No, that wasn't me!

Wait! I have a theory!

Which means, I think I know the answer, obviously.

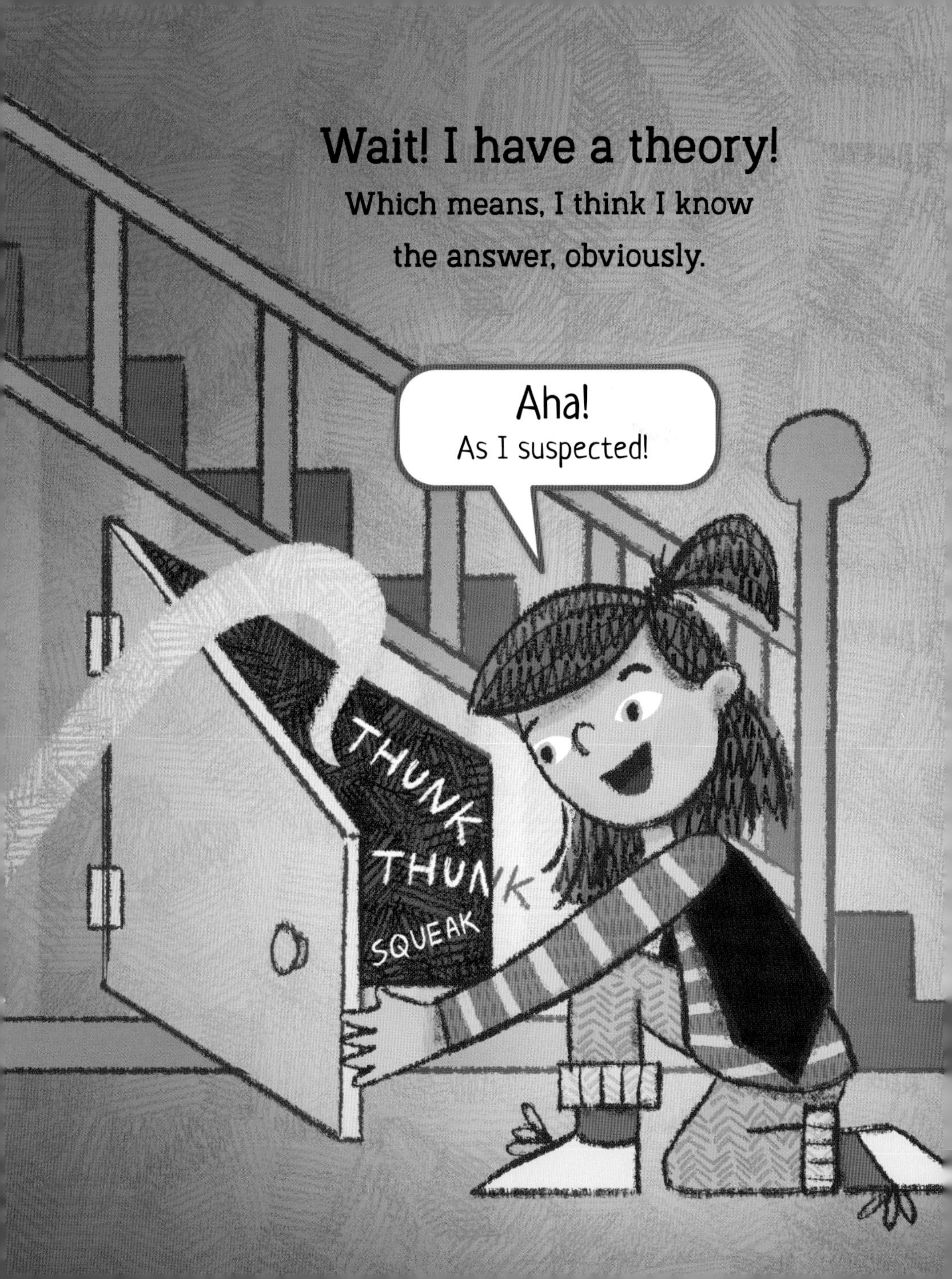
Aha!
As I suspected!
THUNK
THUNK
SQUEAK

A family of musical mice!

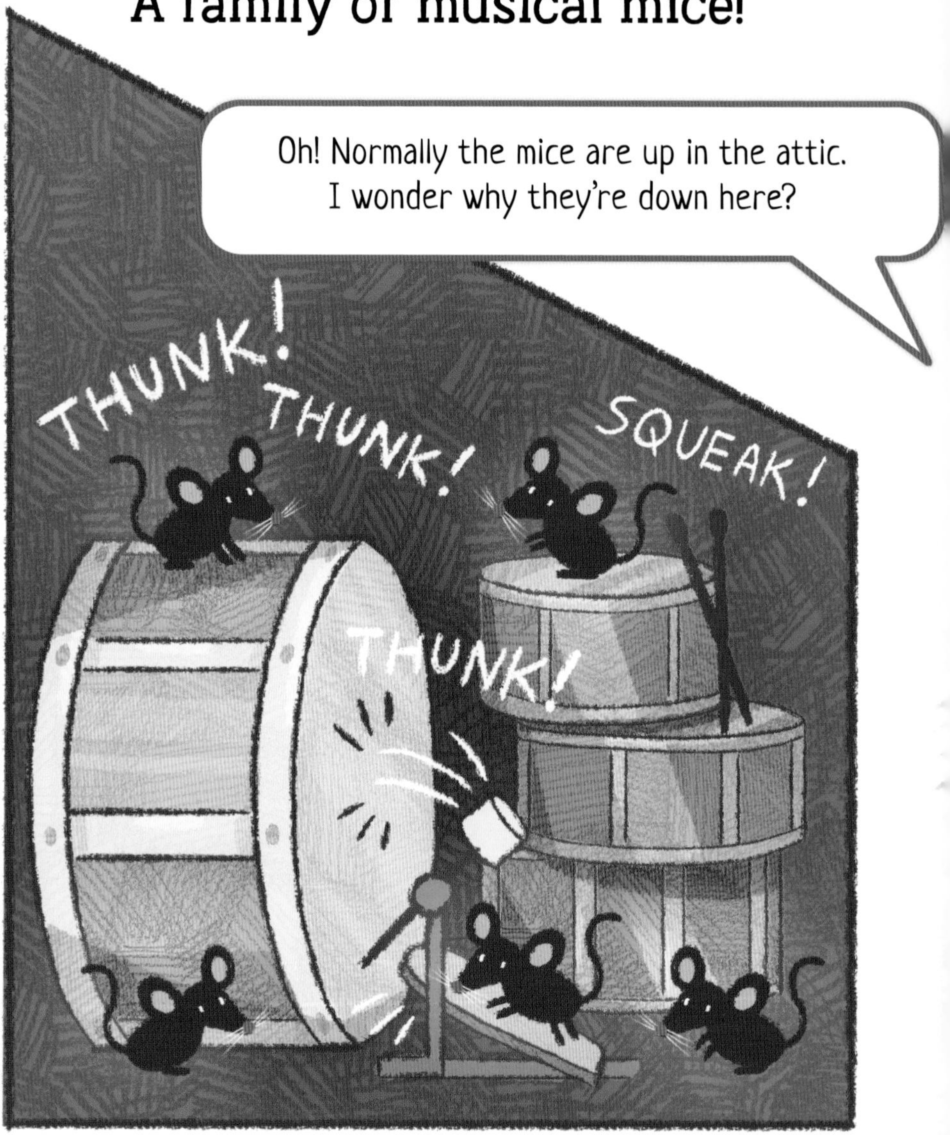
Oh! Normally the mice are up in the attic. I wonder why they're down here?
THUNK!
THUNK!
SQUEAK!
THUNK!

GHOST EVIDENCE

~~Shadowy figures in the front hallway.~~

☑ Neighbor in window.

~~Thumping footsteps on the stairs.~~

☑ Mice thunking on the drums.

— Upstairs doors that shut on their own.

Baby owl?

Chapter Five

The evidence so far has not proven that the Evergreen Street Music School is haunted. But we still have one more investigation to go, so we head upstairs.

Wow! Do haunted houses always look so—

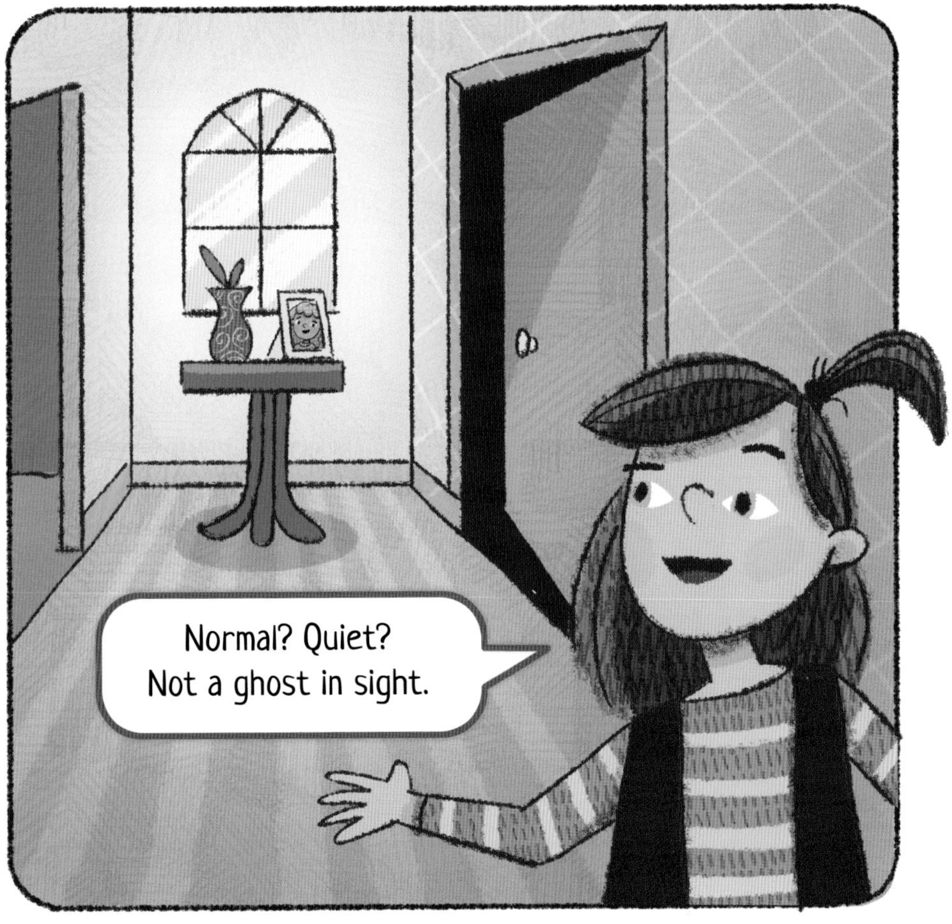
Normal? Quiet?
Not a ghost in sight.

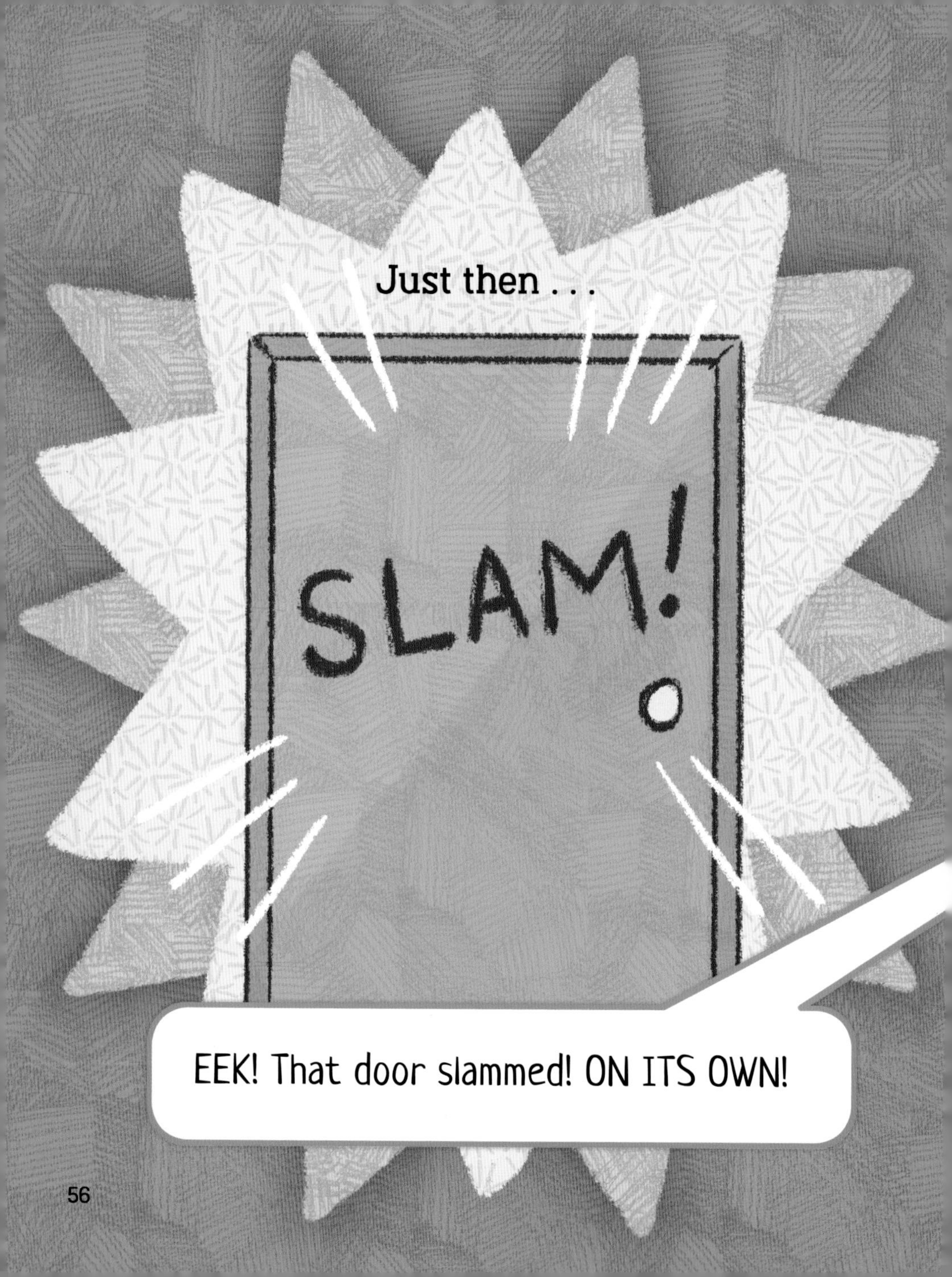
Just then . . .
SLAM!
EEK! That door slammed! ON ITS OWN!

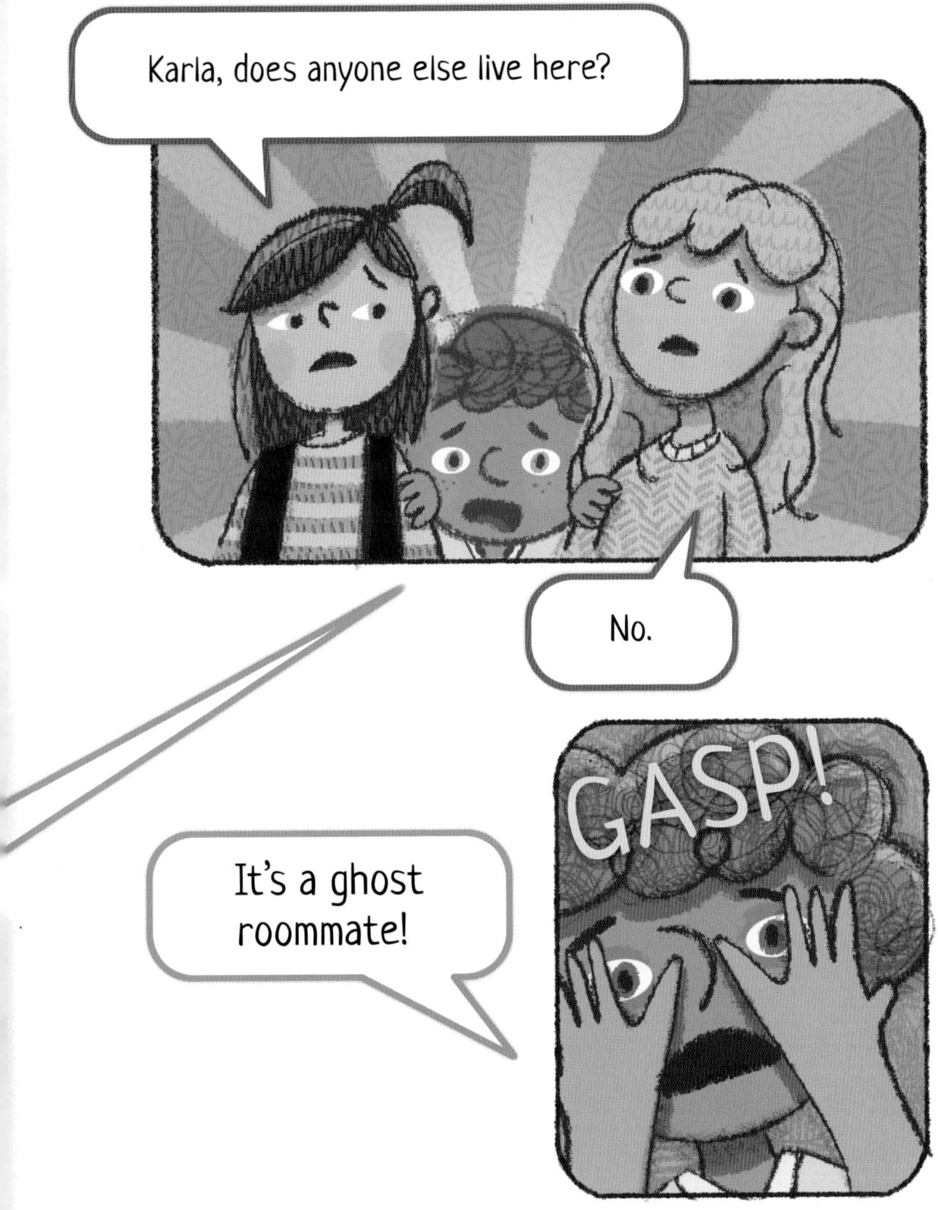
Karla, does anyone else live here?
No.
It's a ghost roommate!
GASP!

When things are confusing,
it can be scary.
The best way to face fear is
to focus on the facts!

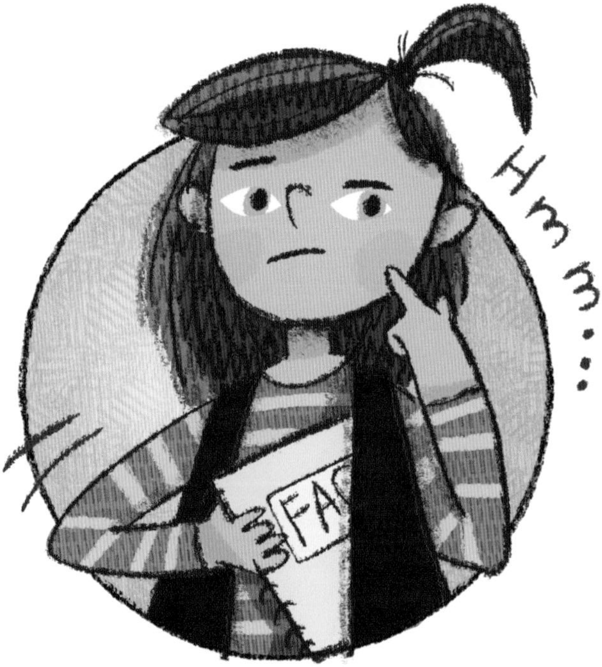
Hmm...
FAC

I take a deep breath and write down my observations.

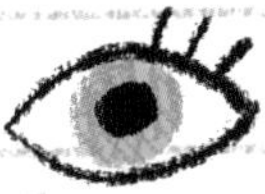

I SAW . . . the door swing shut.

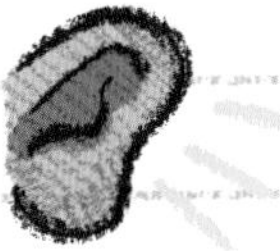

I HEARD . . . it make a loud slam.

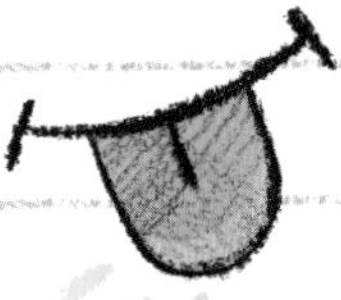

I TASTE . . . bile* in my mouth, which means I'm nervous!

*Bile: a fluid in your body that might give you a sour taste, if your tummy is upset from being nervous.

Yes, even Fact Collectors get nervous.
But doors don't close without something or someone closing them. I need to check out this door.

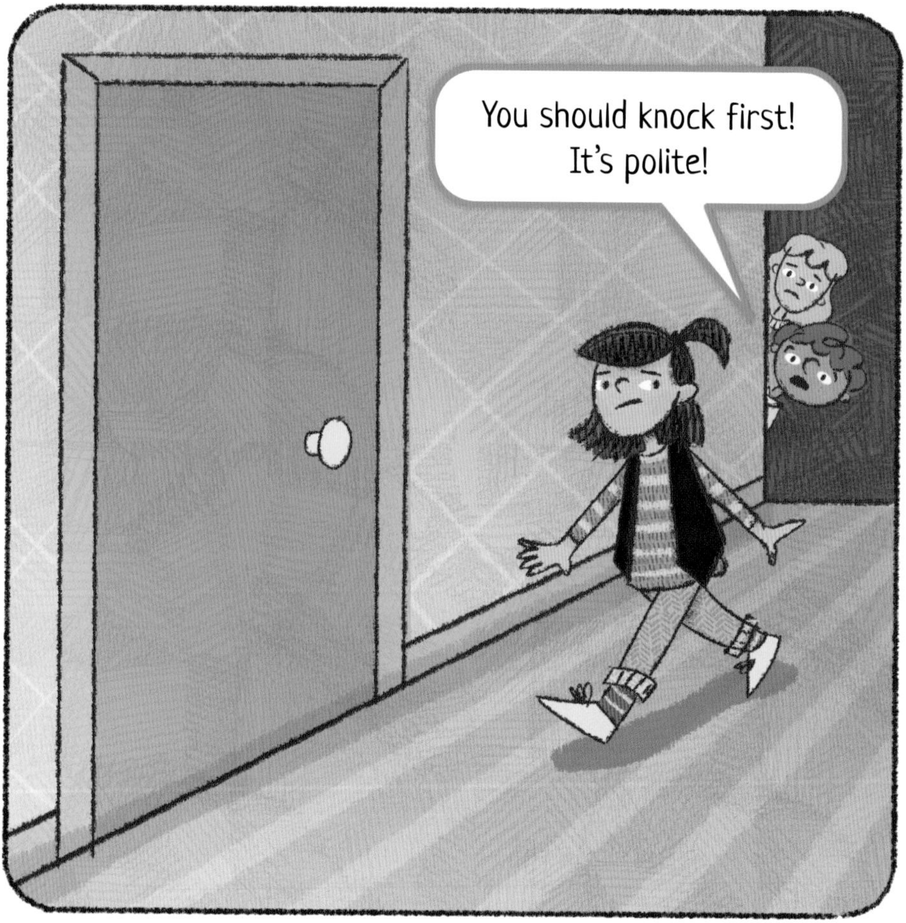
You should knock first! It's polite!

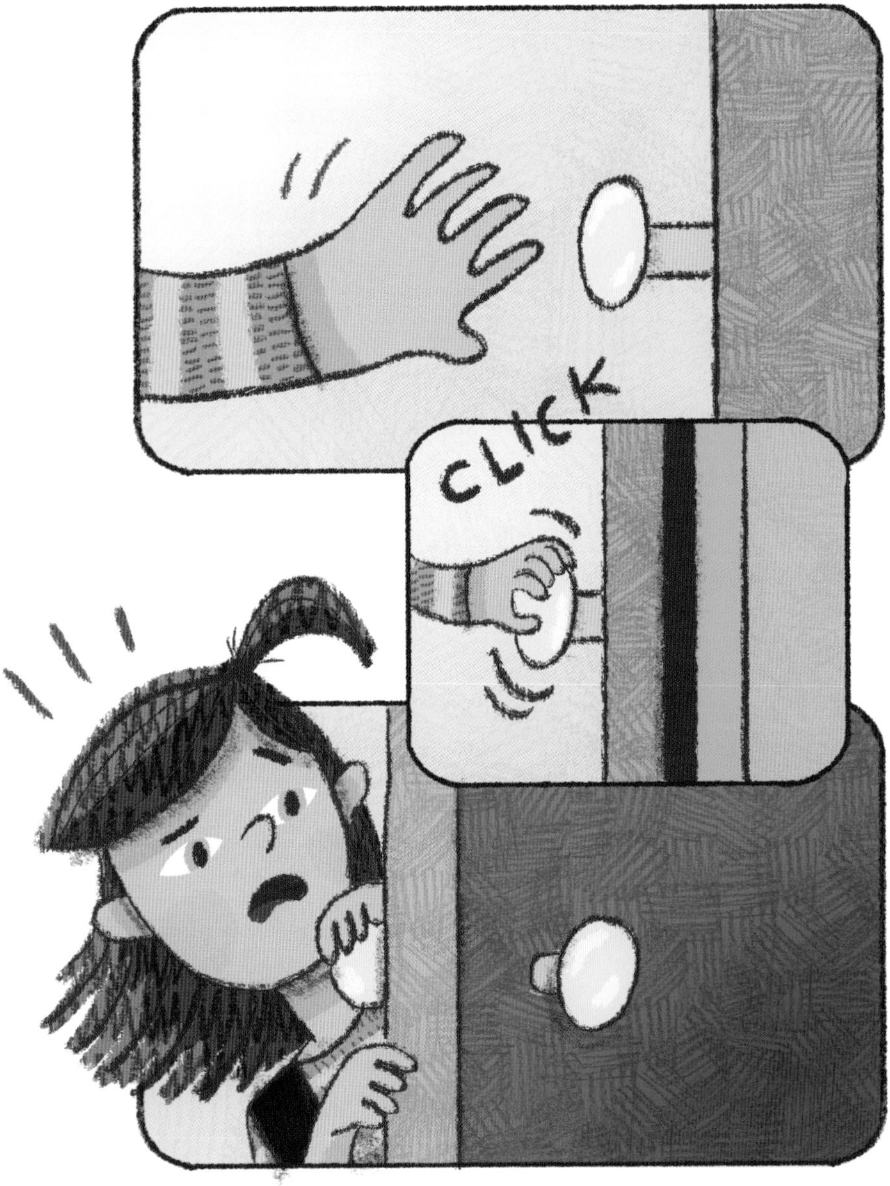
CLICK

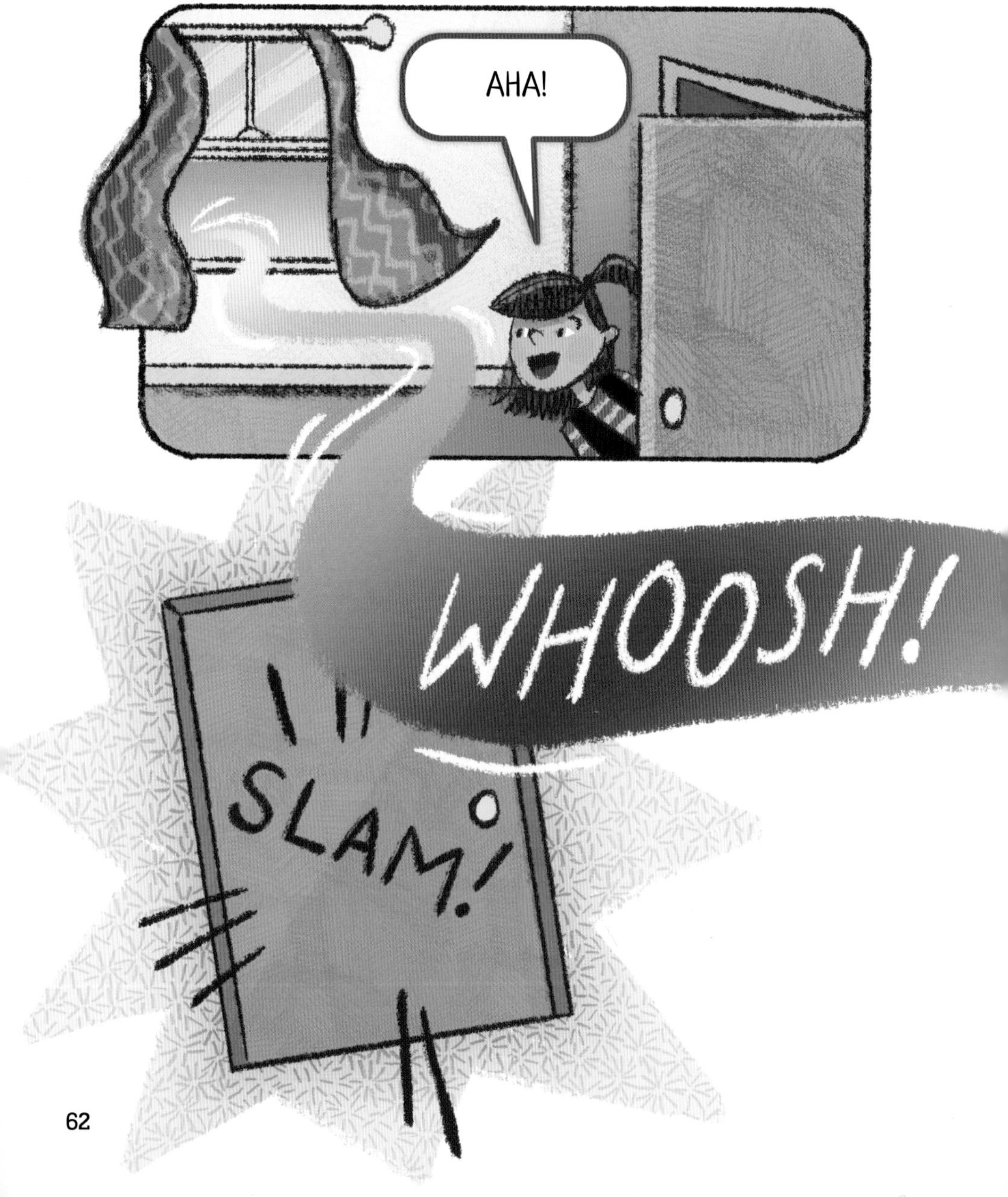
AHA!
WHOOSH!
SLAM!

Now I see it. It's a window that is wide open!

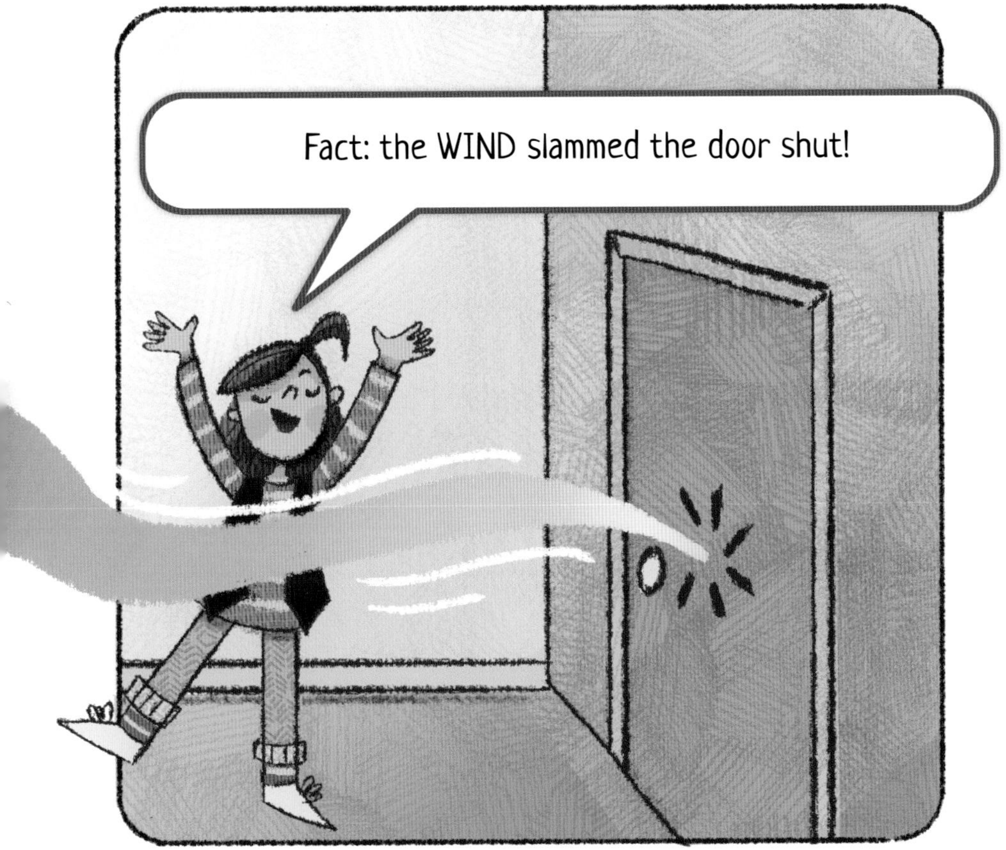
Fact: the WIND slammed the door shut!

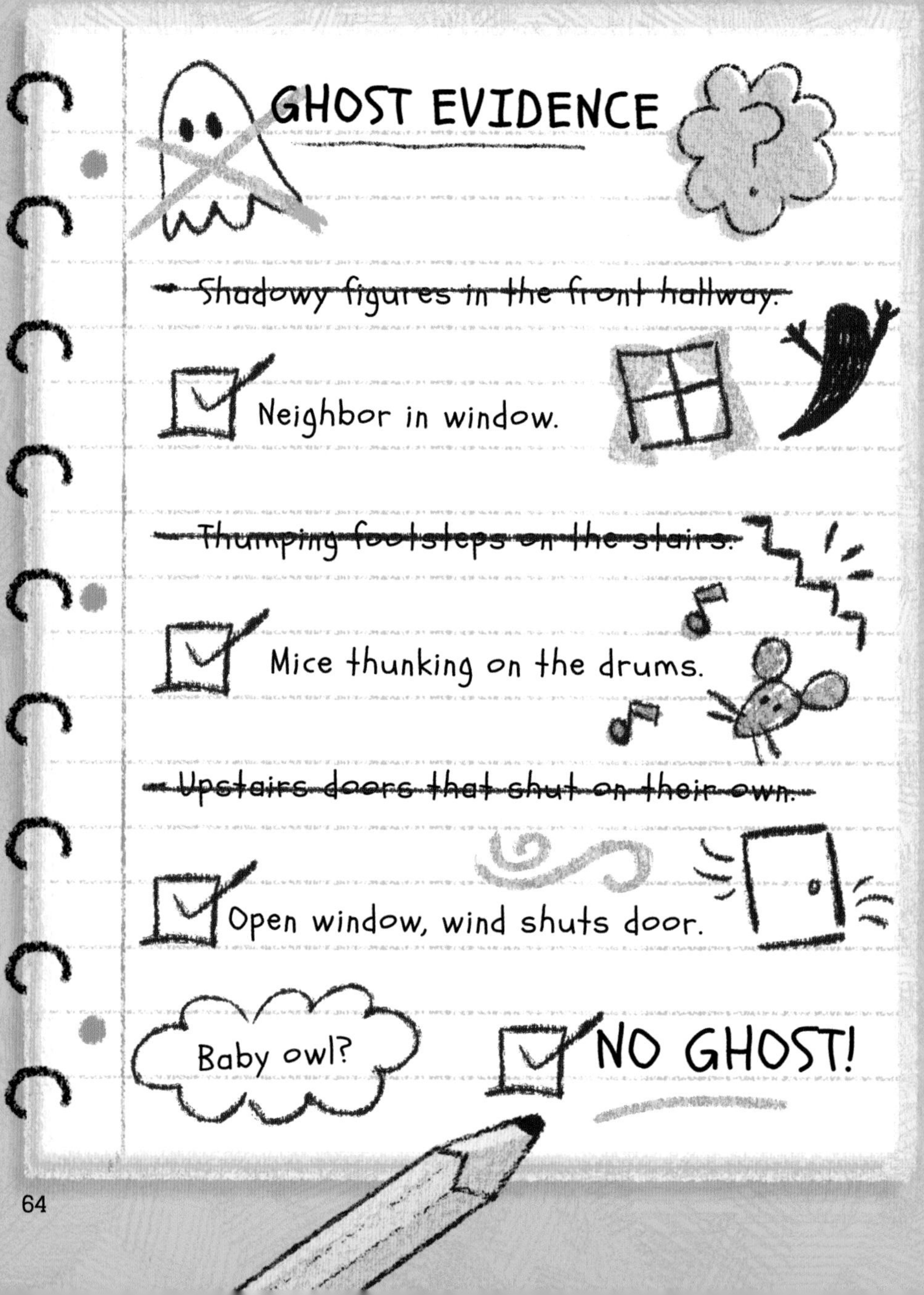
GHOST EVIDENCE
~~Shadowy figures in the front hallway.~~
Neighbor in window.
~~Thumping footsteps on the stairs.~~
Mice thunking on the drums.
~~Upstairs doors that shut on their own.~~
Open window, wind shuts door.
Baby owl?
NO GHOST!

Chapter Six

I have done it!

I, Paige, talented Fact Collector,

have proven a fact!

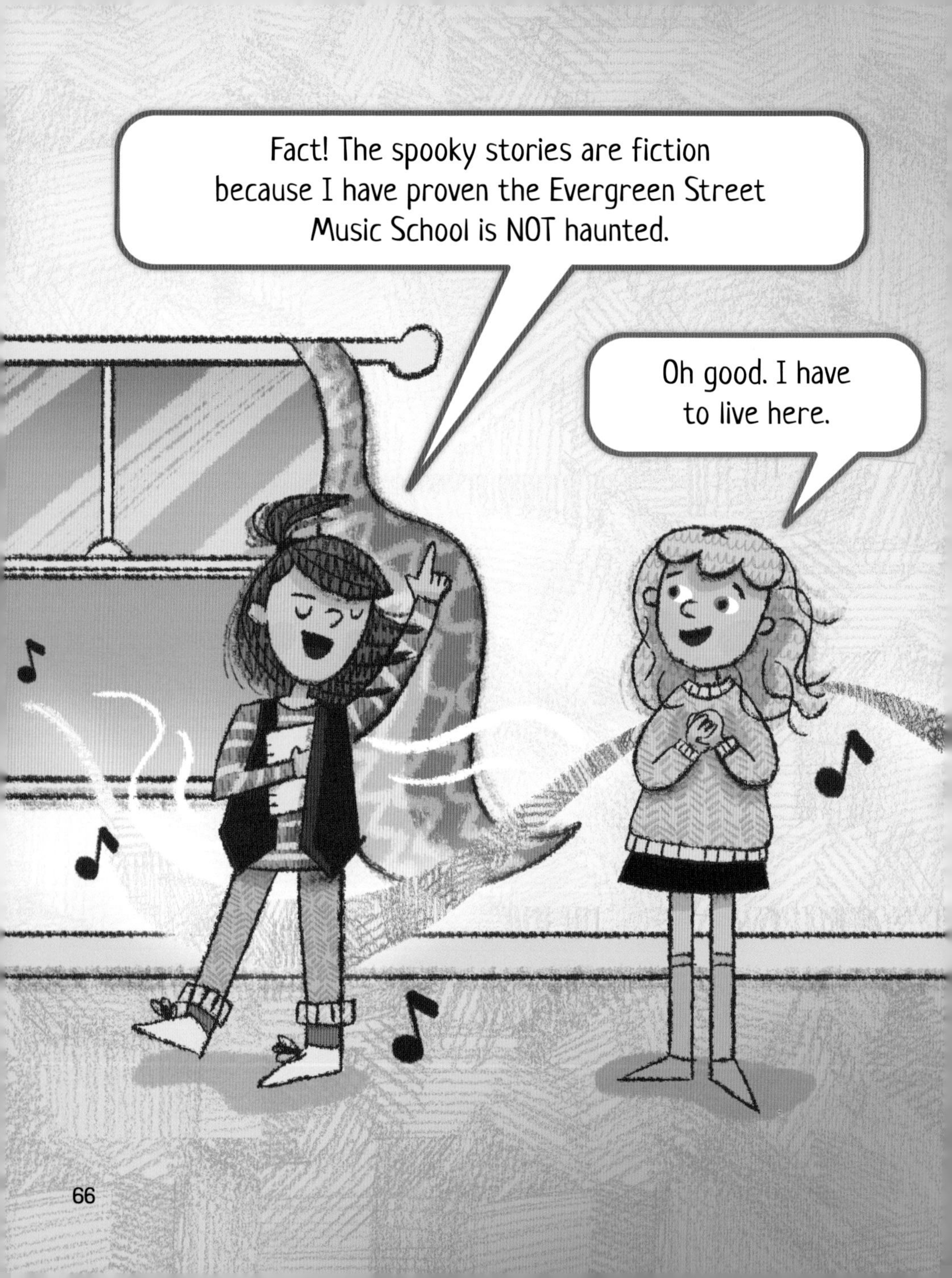
Fact! The spooky stories are fiction because I have proven the Evergreen Street Music School is NOT haunted.
Oh good. I have to live here.

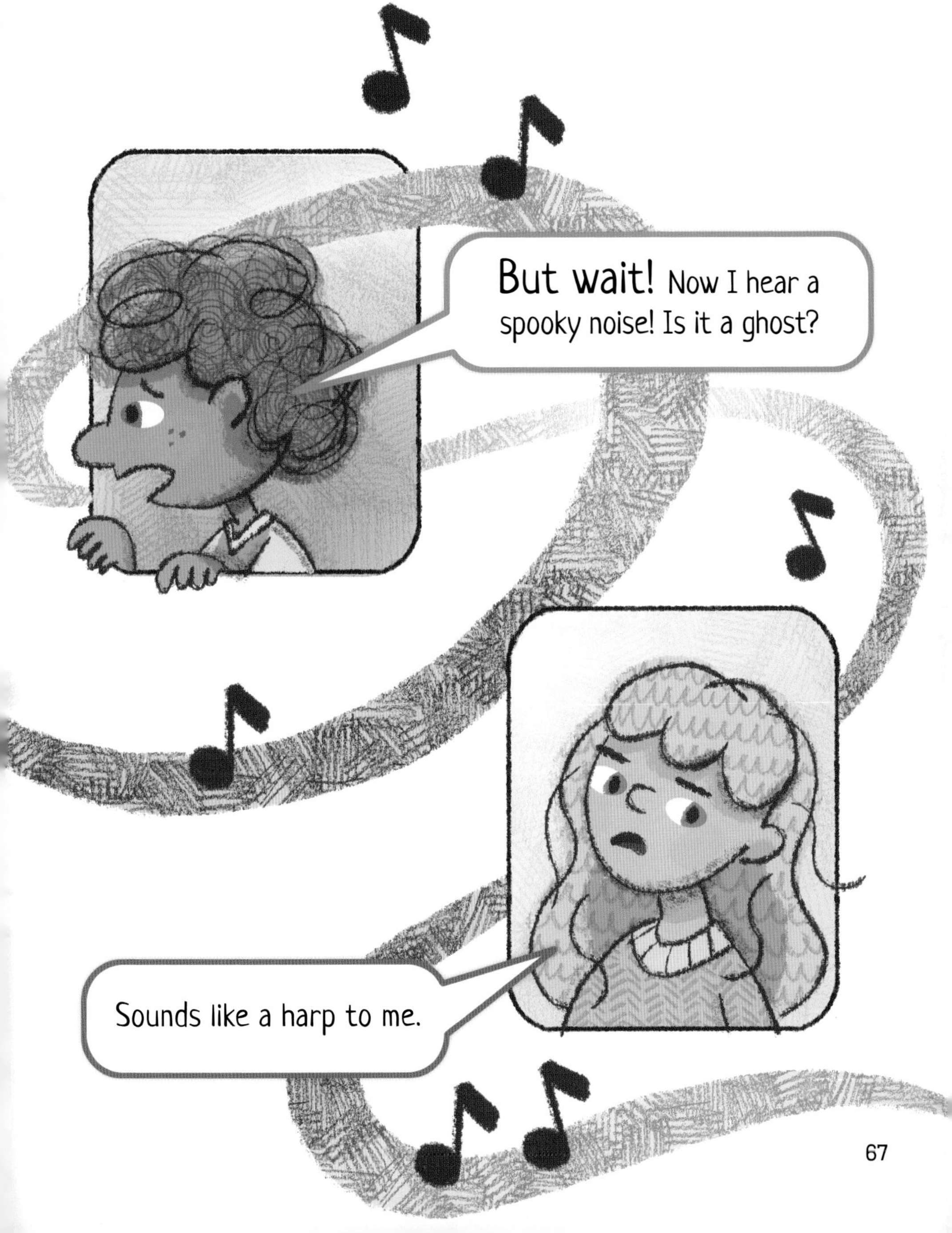
But wait! Now I hear a spooky noise! Is it a ghost?
Sounds like a harp to me.

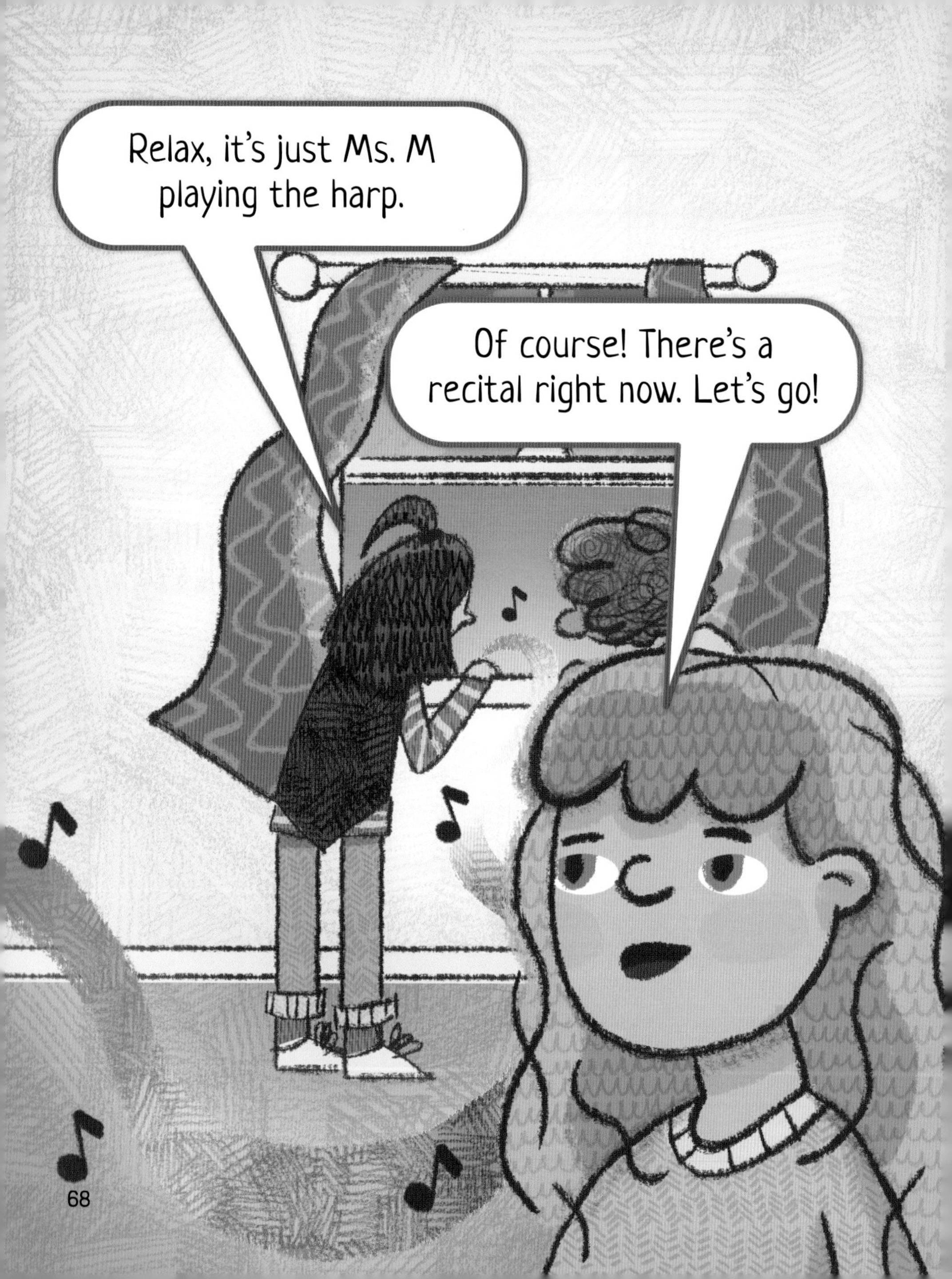
Relax, it's just Ms. M playing the harp.
Of course! There's a recital right now. Let's go!

We head outside.

A relaxing music recital seems like a great way to celebrate an afternoon of difficult fact proving.

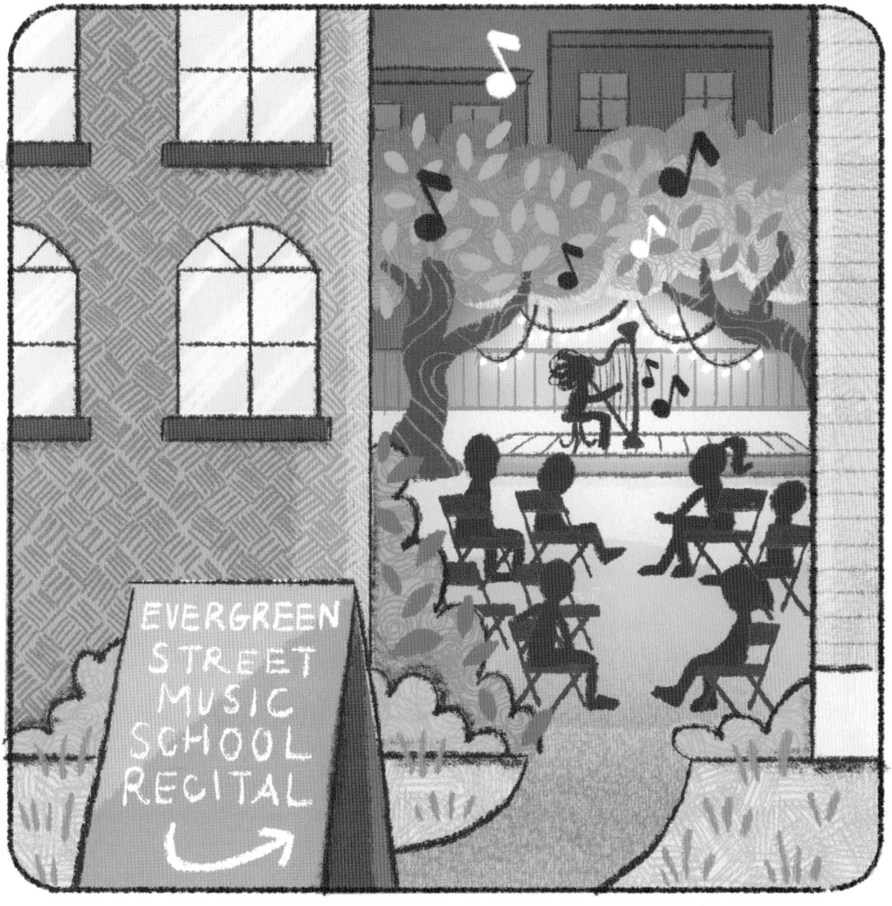
EVERGREEN
STREET
MUSIC
SCHOOL
RECITAL

We like listening to Ms. M's harp,

and Mr. Drufus and his whistling birds,

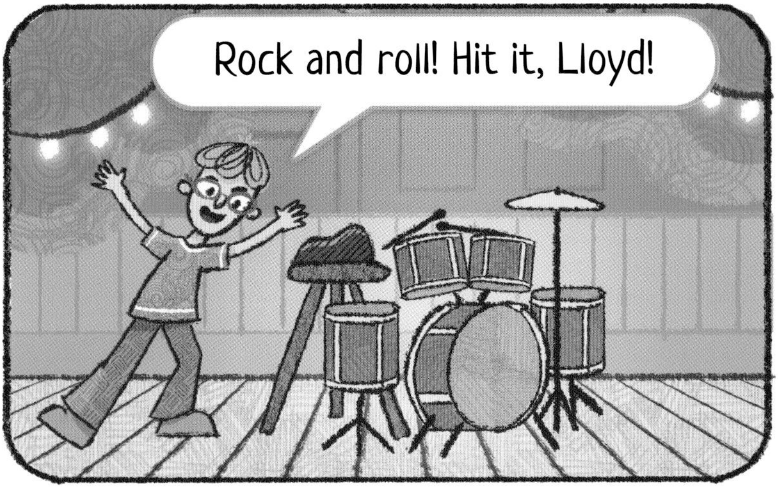
Rock and roll! Hit it, Lloyd!

and the rock . . .

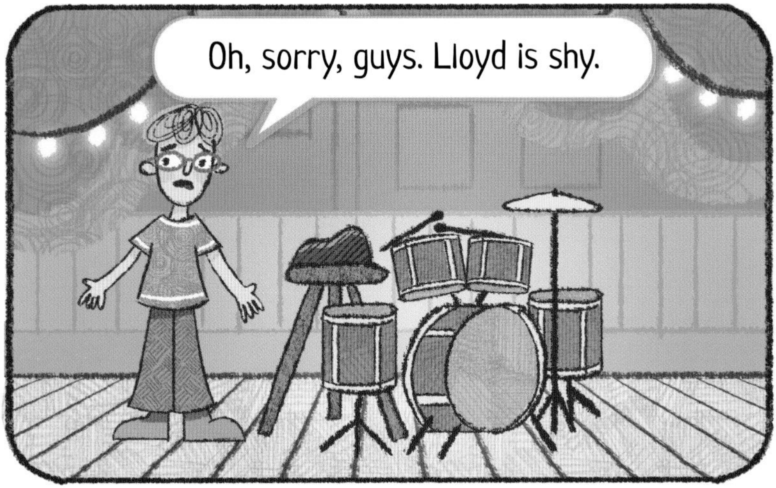
Oh, sorry, guys. Lloyd is shy.

Karla's grandma plays the piano.

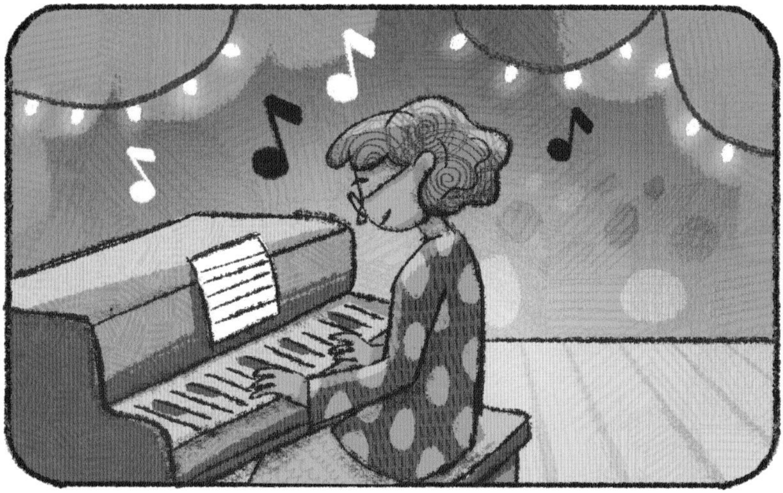

I'm enjoying it, but Penn keeps fidgeting.

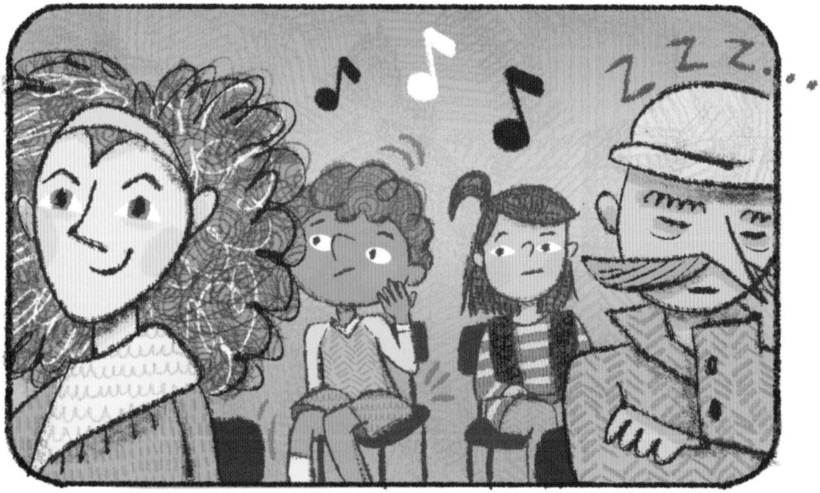
Z Z Z...

He looks
to the side . . .

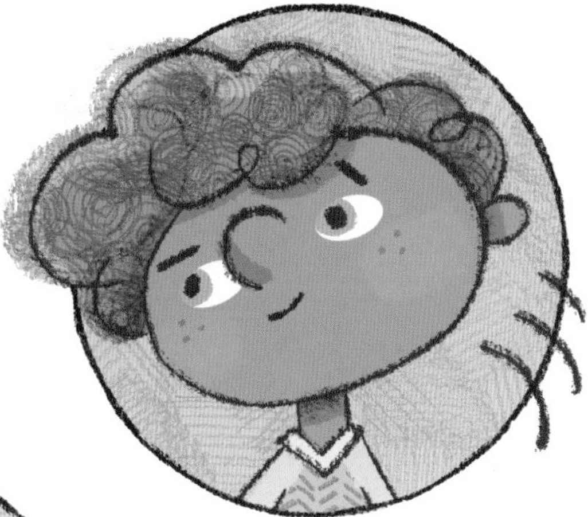

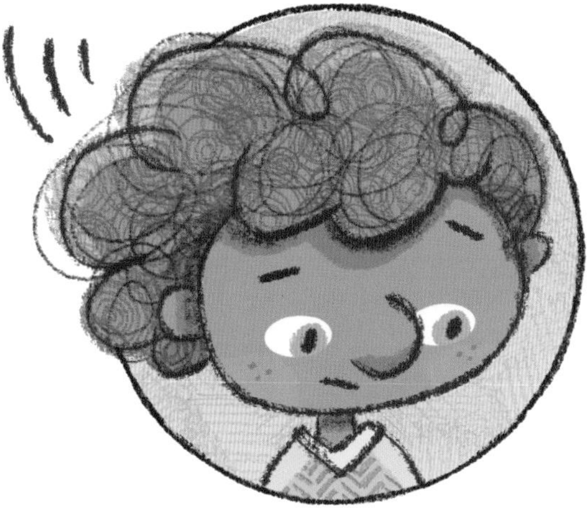

He looks down . . .

He looks up,
and then . . .

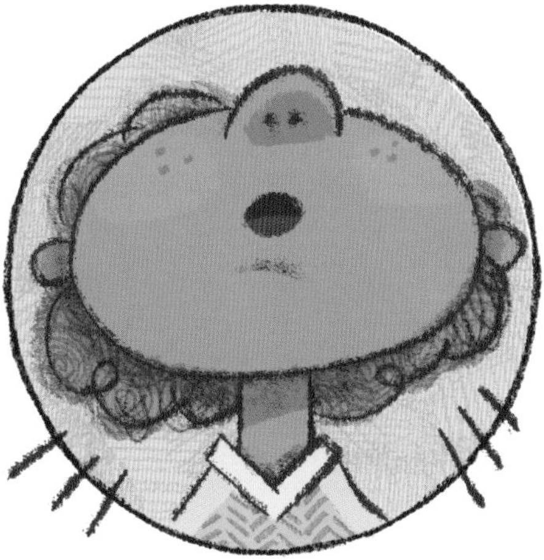

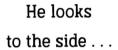

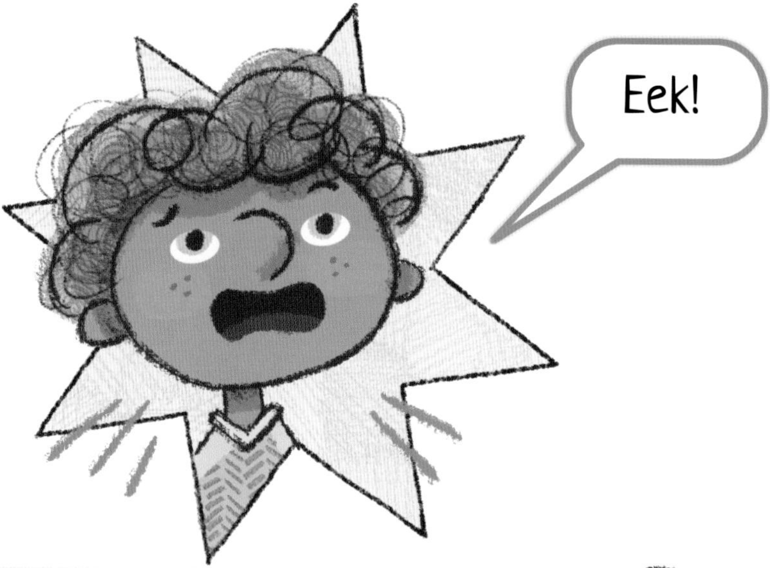
Eek!

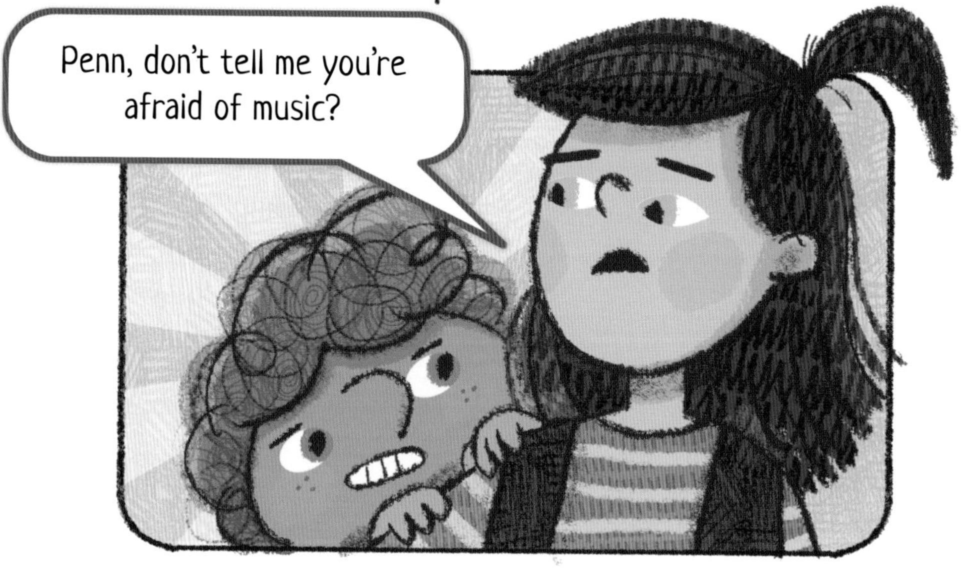
Penn, don't tell me you're afraid of music?

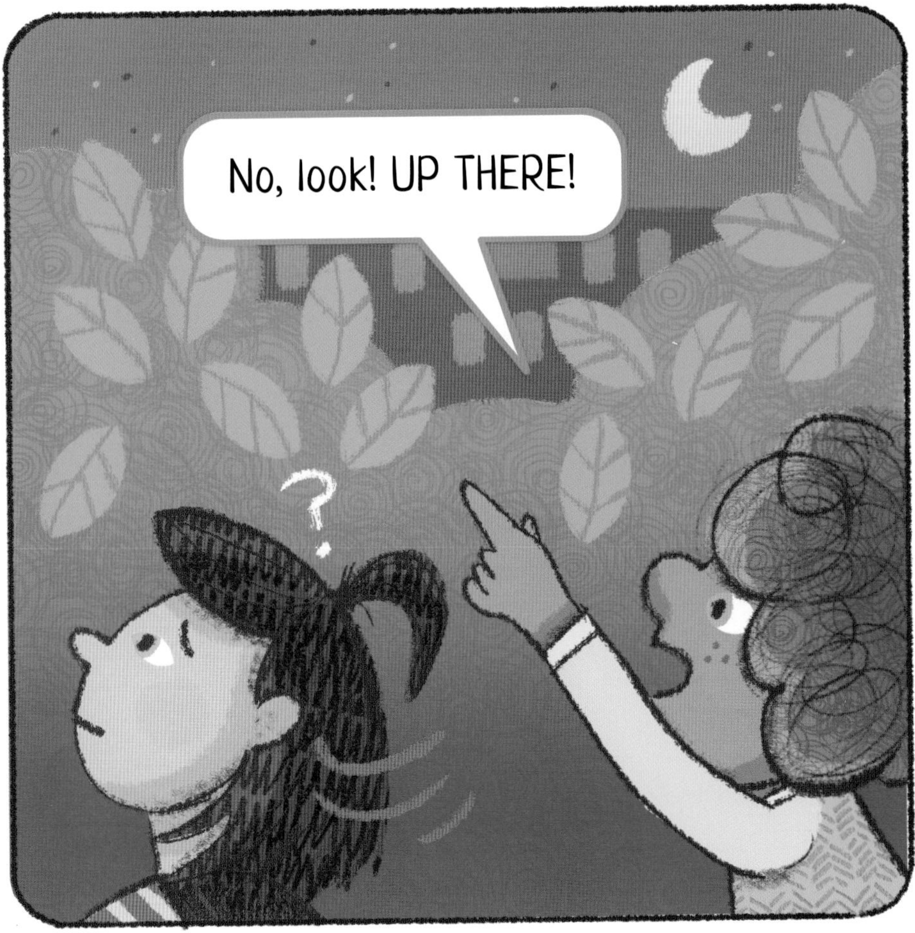
No, look! UP THERE!

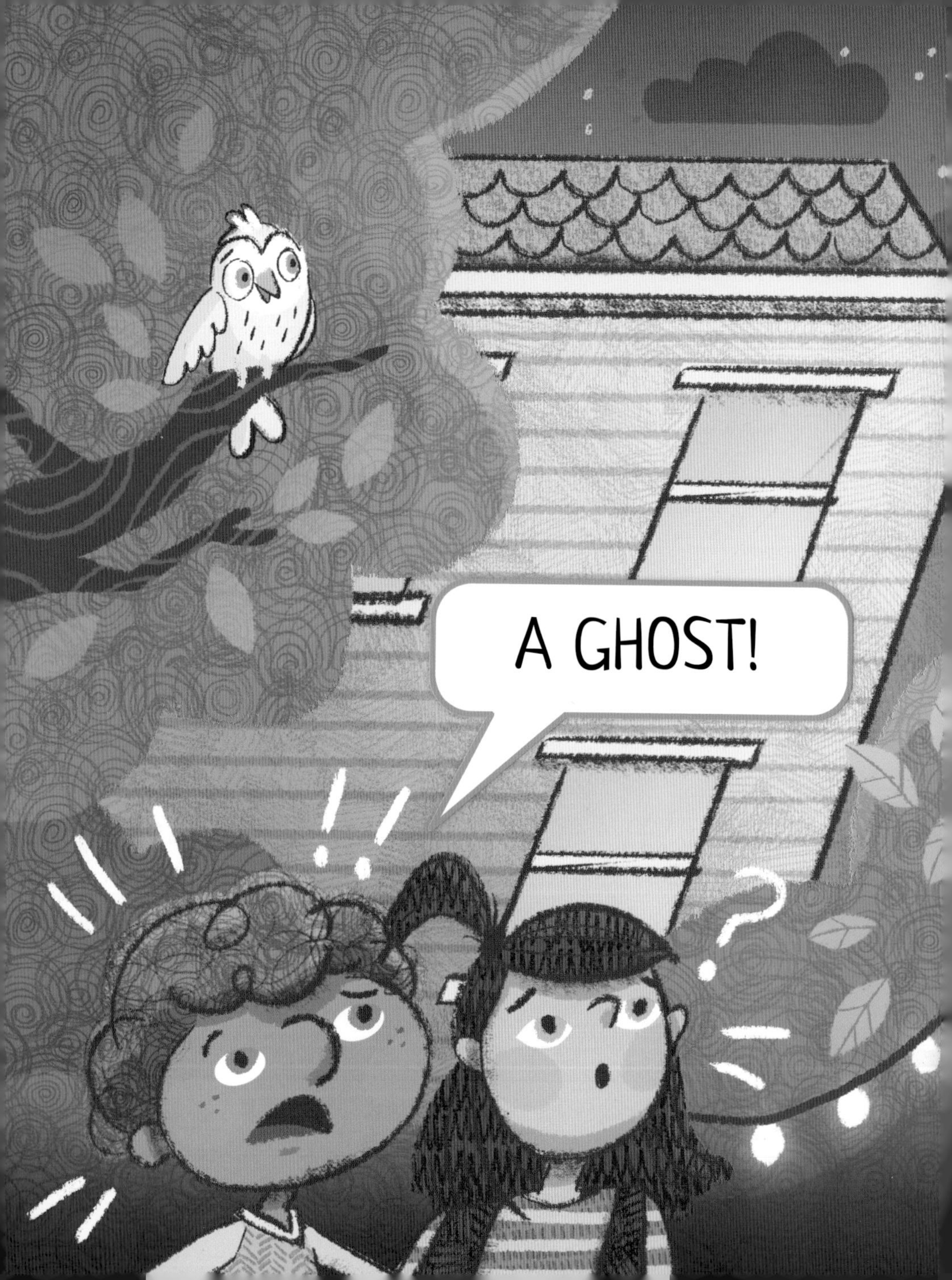
A GHOST!

Chapter Seven

If someone says something,
that doesn't make it a fact.
But what about if you see something?

Fact: The human eye can see about ten million colors.

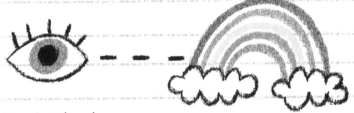

Fact: The human eye can see about the distance of two miles.

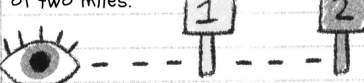

There are no facts about the human eye seeing ghosts in attic windows, as far as I know.

Even after a fact is proven,
new evidence showing up means
you need to re-prove the fact.

Sometimes this even
changes the proven fact!

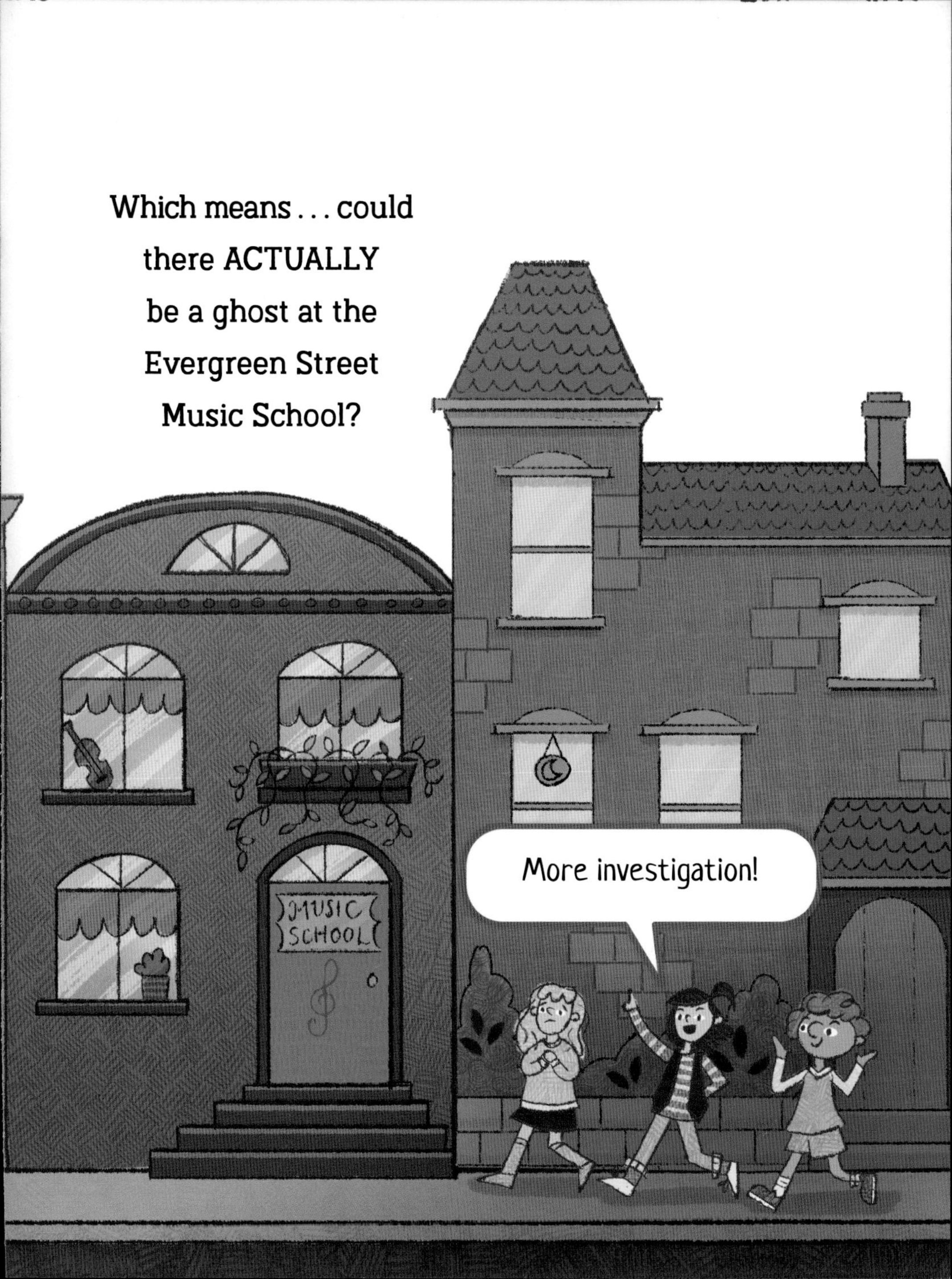
Which means . . . could there ACTUALLY be a ghost at the Evergreen Street Music School?
MUSIC SCHOOL
More investigation!

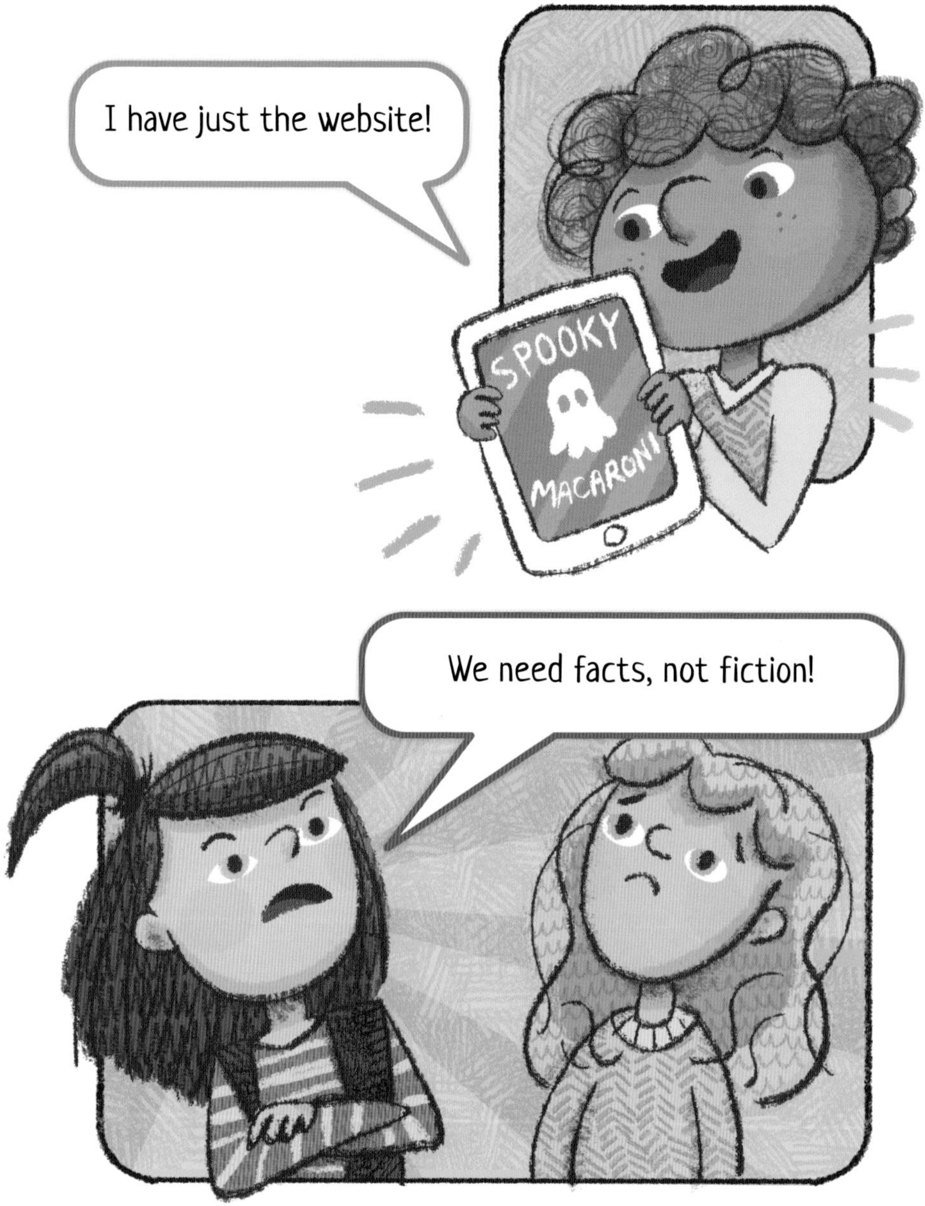
I have just the website!
SPOOKY MACARONI
We need facts, not fiction!

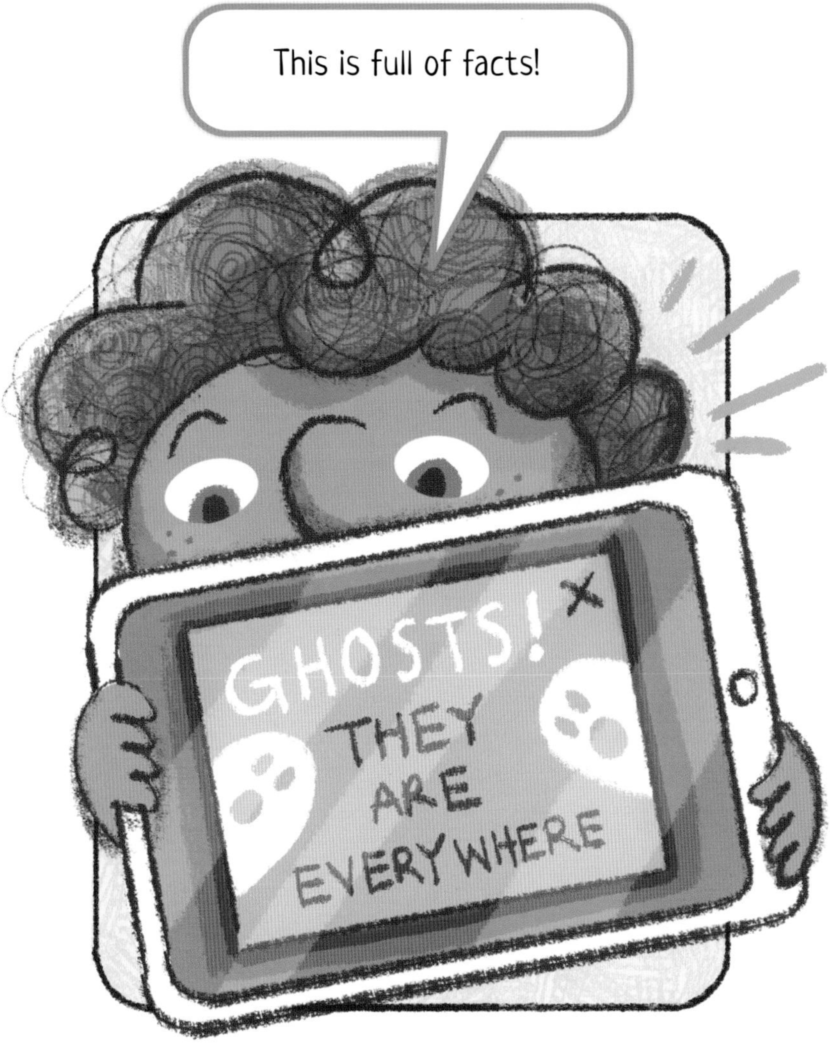
This is full of facts!
GHOSTS!
THEY ARE EVERYWHERE

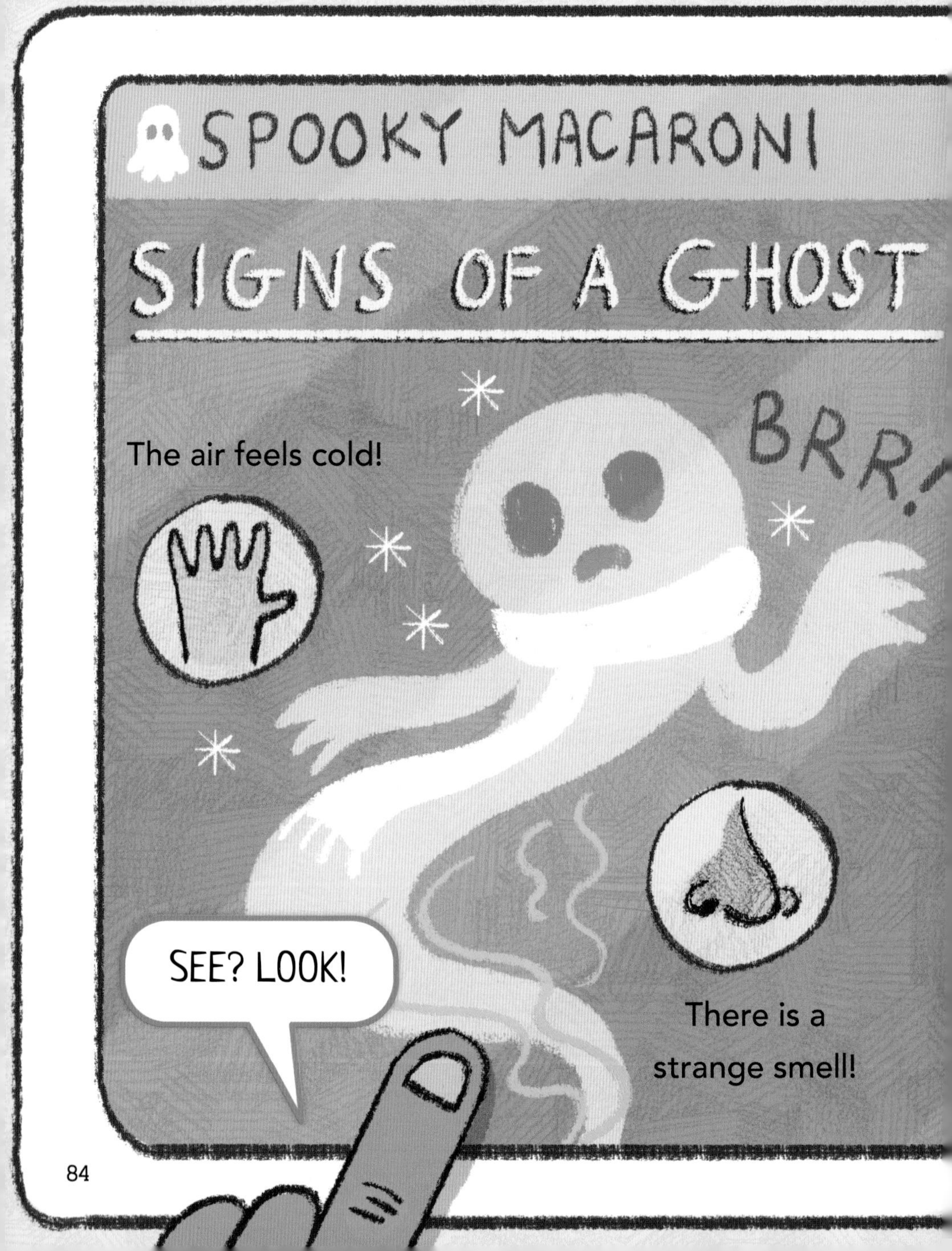
SPOOKY MACARONI
SIGNS OF A GHOST
The air feels cold!
BRR!
There is a strange smell!
SEE? LOOK!

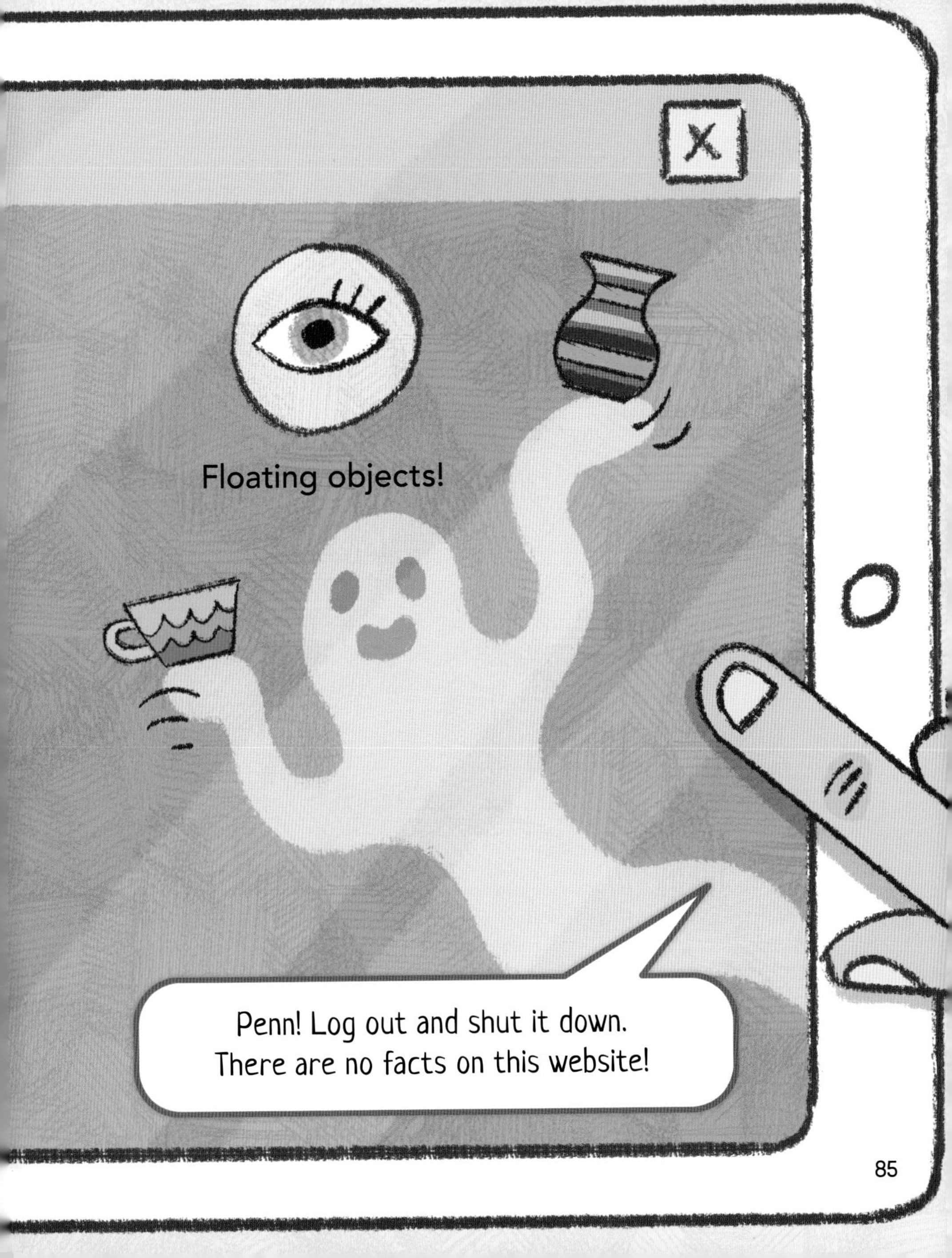
X
Floating objects!
Penn! Log out and shut it down.
There are no facts on this website!

I'm not so sure about all this ghost nonsense.

It seems like Karla isn't either.

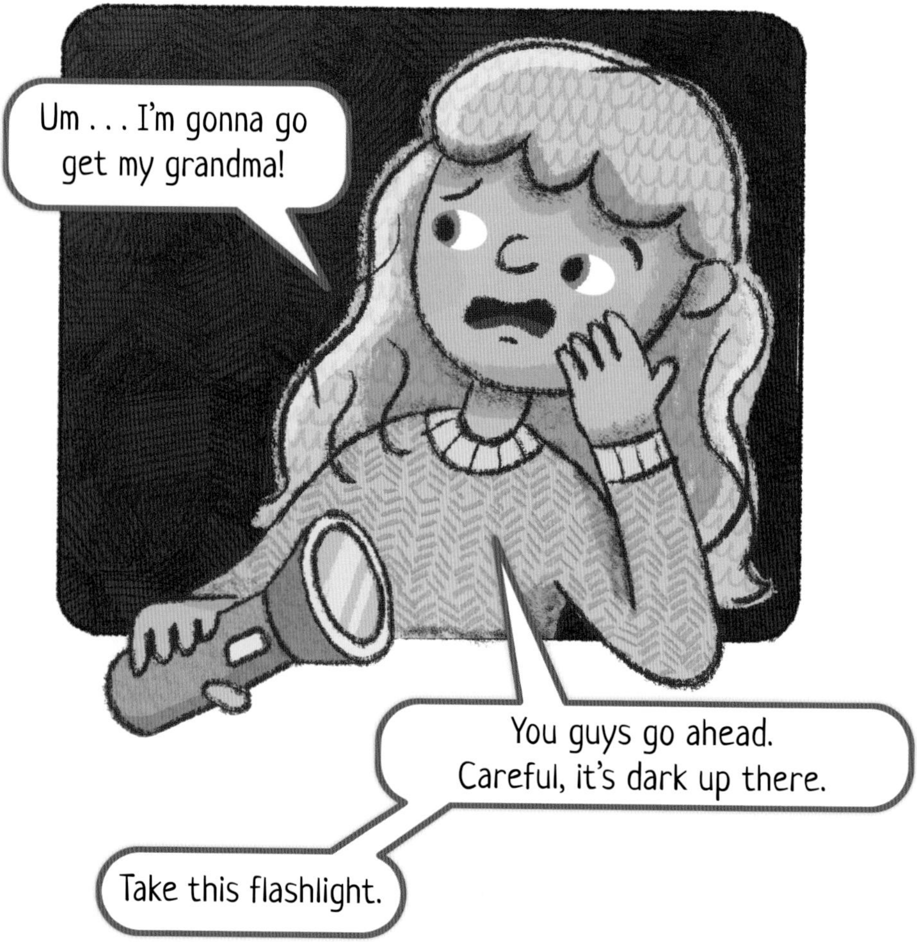
Um . . . I'm gonna go get my grandma!
You guys go ahead. Careful, it's dark up there.
Take this flashlight.

So we go ahead, right up into the attic!

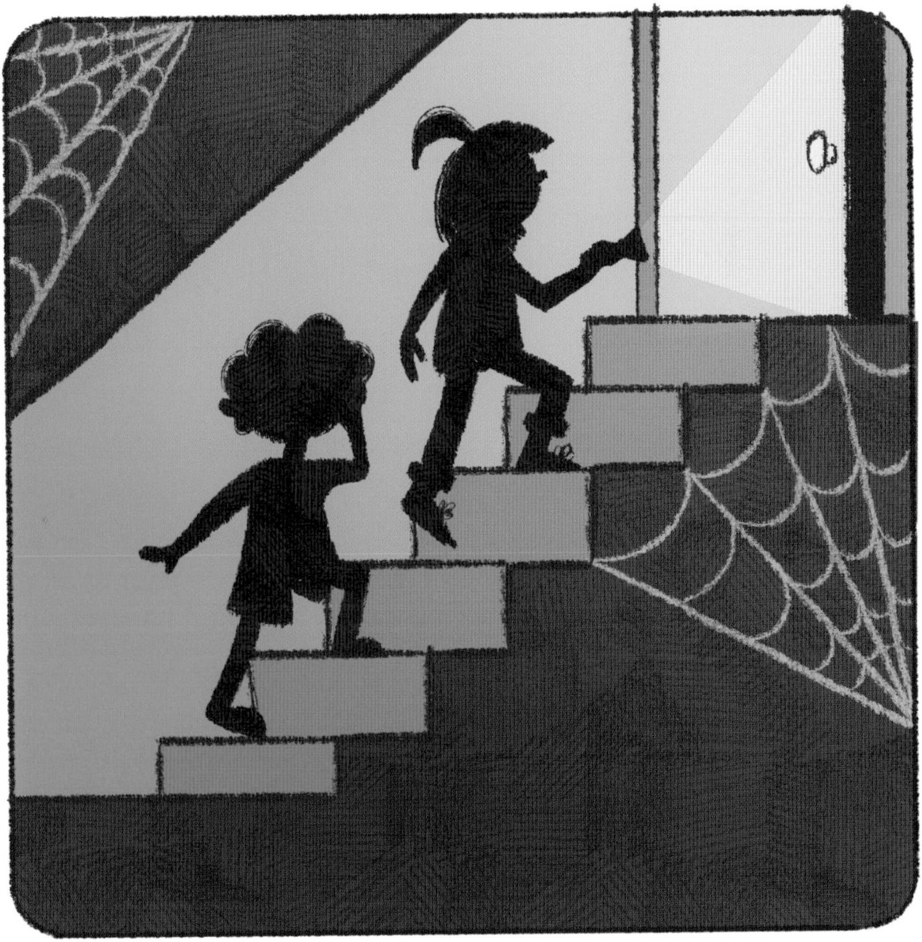

Chapter Eight

The attic above the Evergreen Street Music School definitely looks spooky.

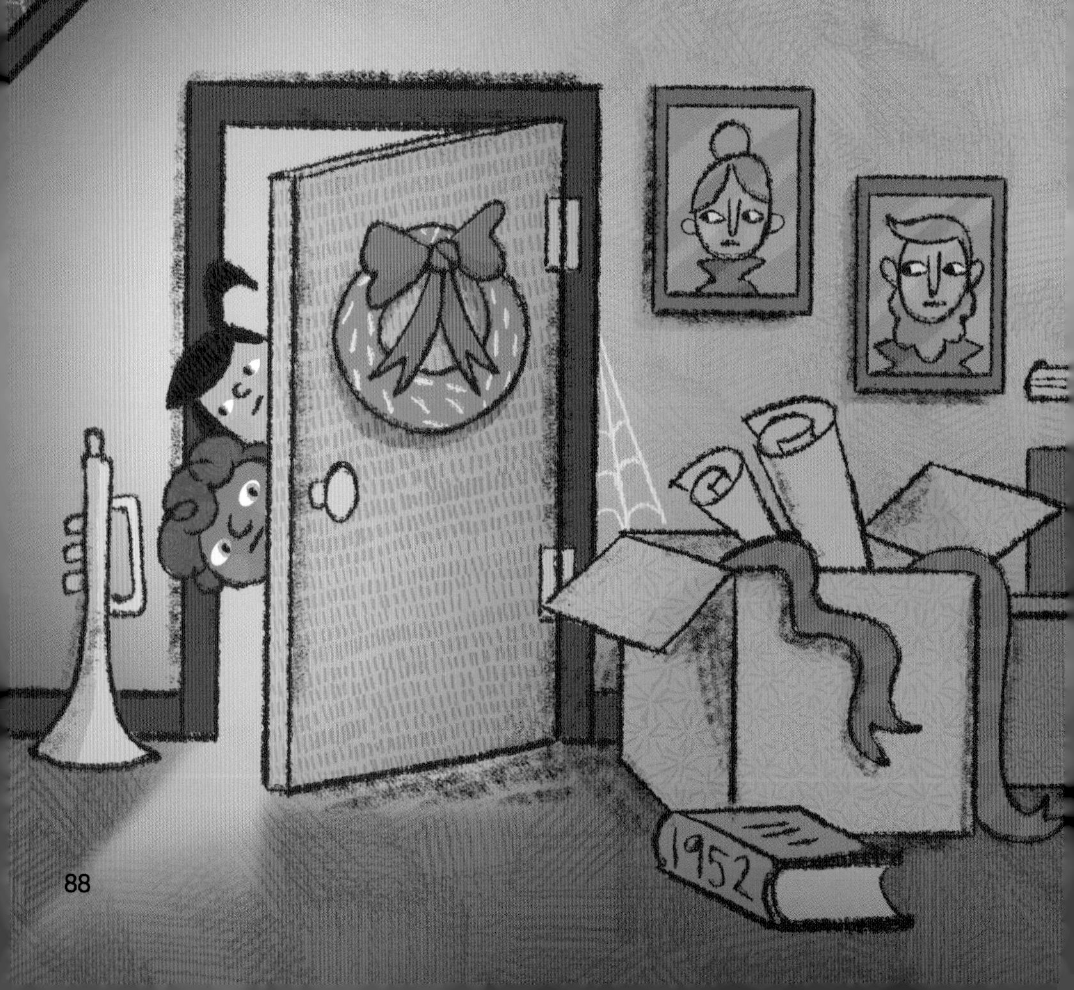
1952

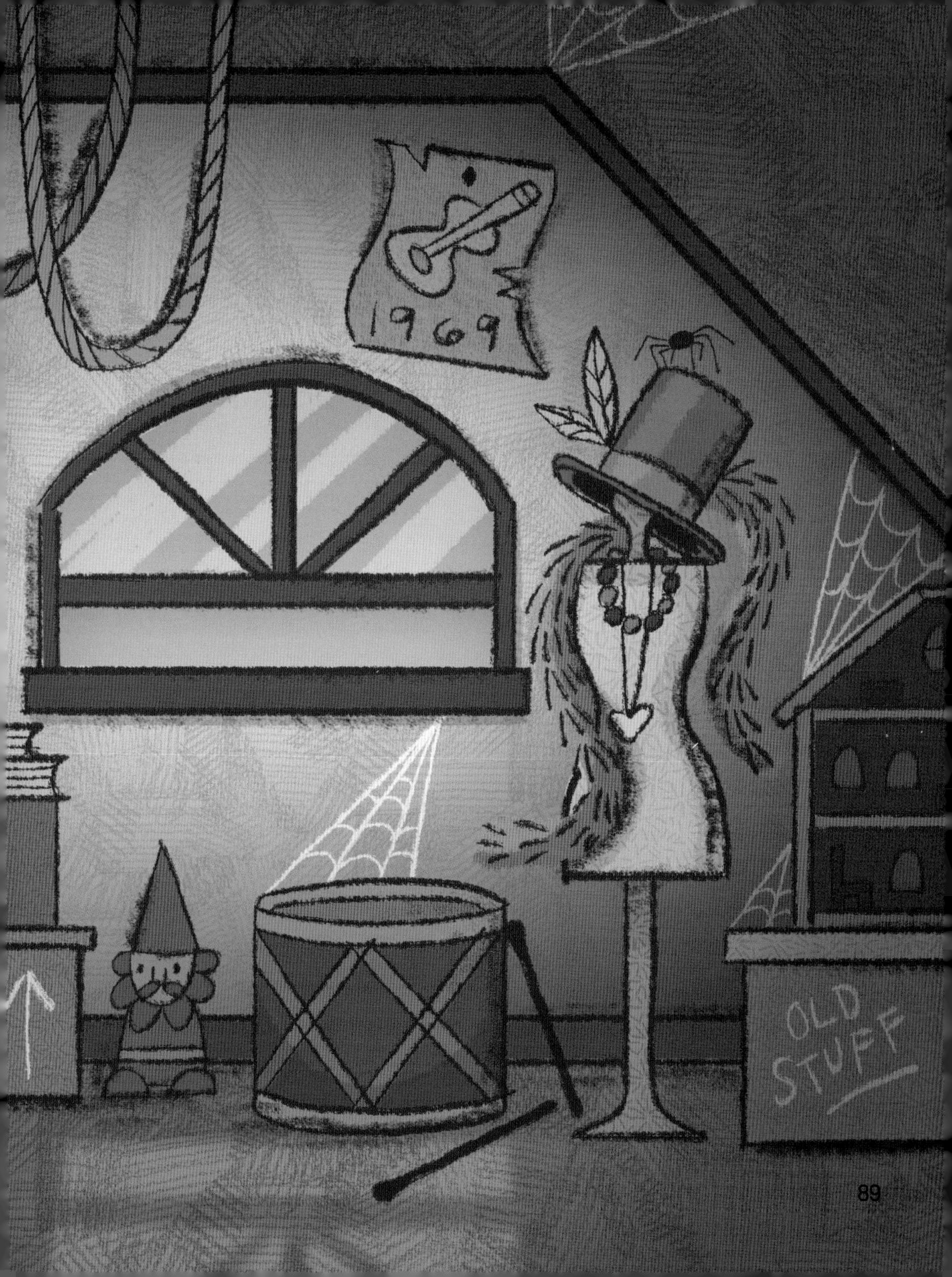
1969
OLD STUFF

But if there is one thing I have learned from my observations, it's that things are not always what they first seem. You need to investigate closer.

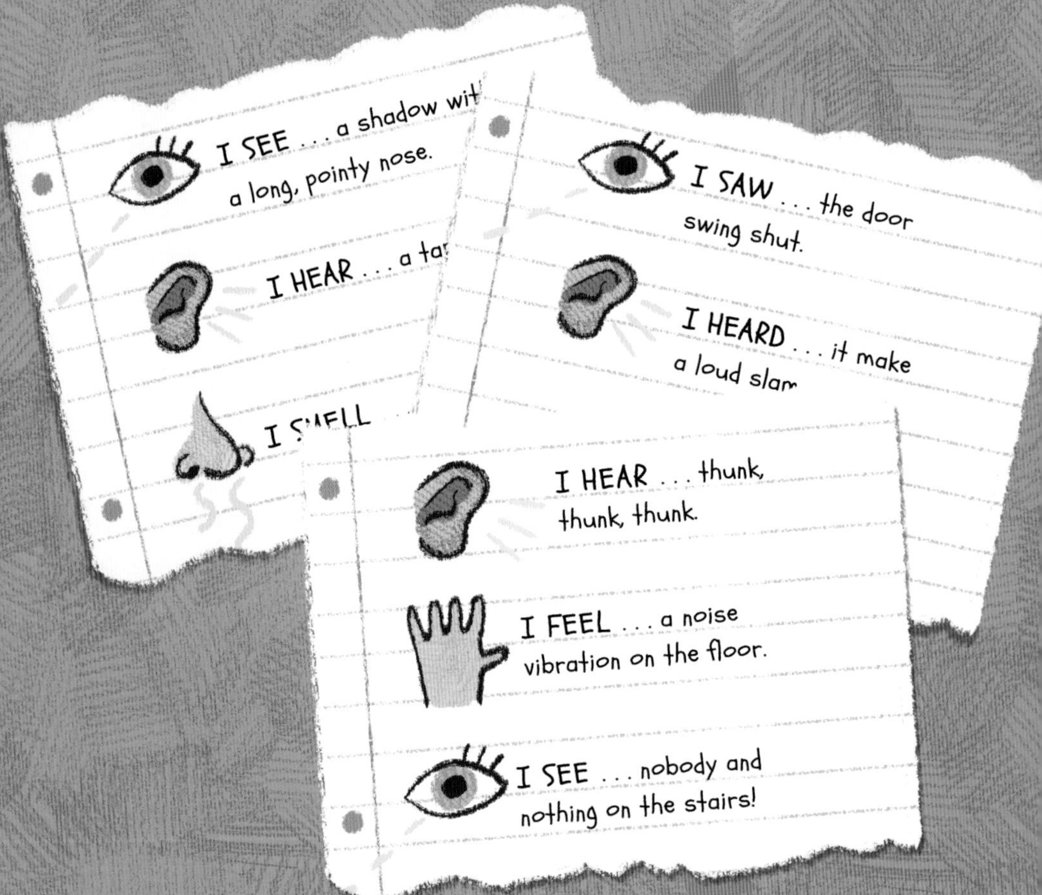

I SEE . . . a shadow wit
a long, pointy nose.
I HEAR . . . a ta
I SMELL
I SAW . . . the door swing shut.
I HEARD . . . it make a loud slam
I HEAR . . . thunk, thunk, thunk.
I FEEL . . . a noise vibration on the floor.
I SEE . . . nobody and nothing on the stairs!

So we walk into the attic. And Penn yelled!

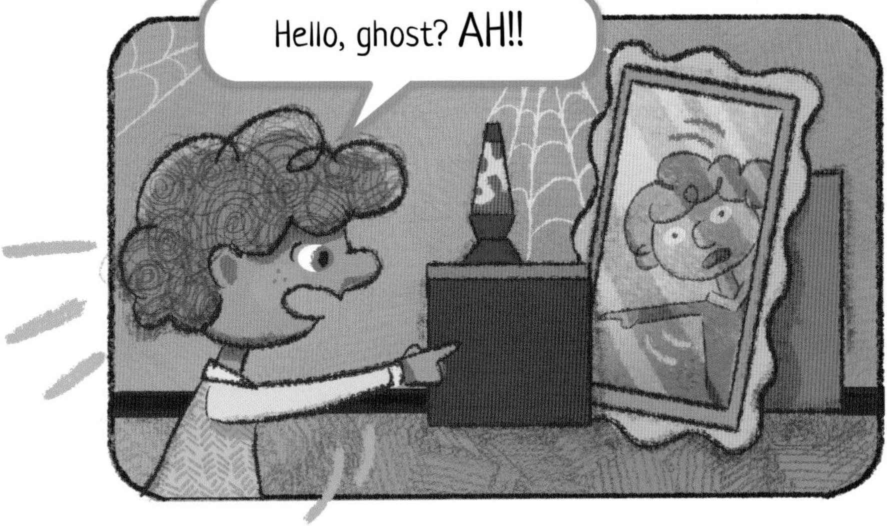
Hello, ghost? AH!!

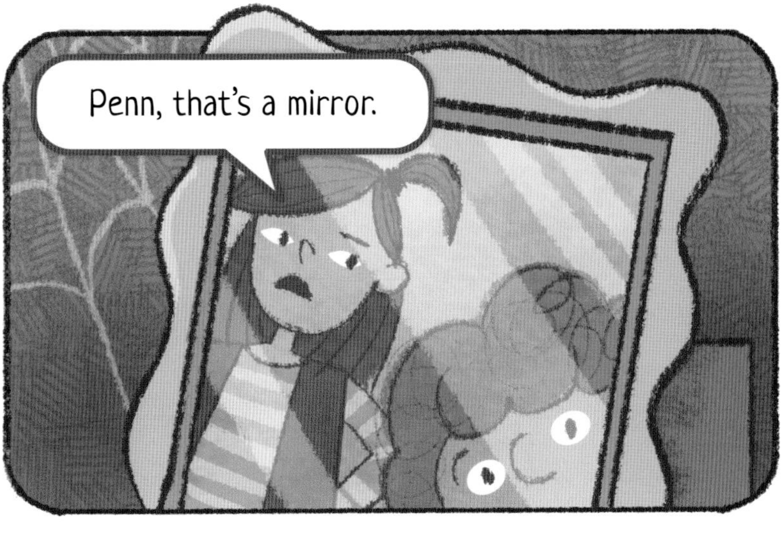
Penn, that's a mirror.

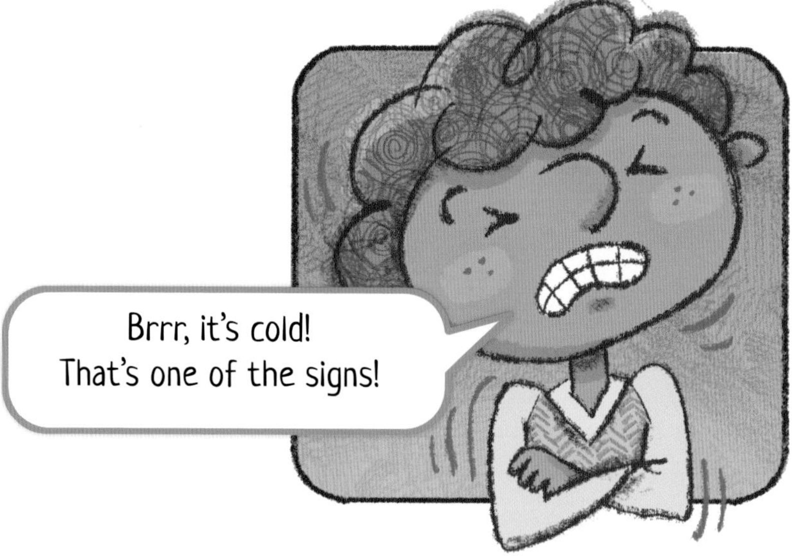
Brrr, it's cold!
That's one of the signs!

It IS cold. When I walk toward the window, I feel that there's a draft coming from it.

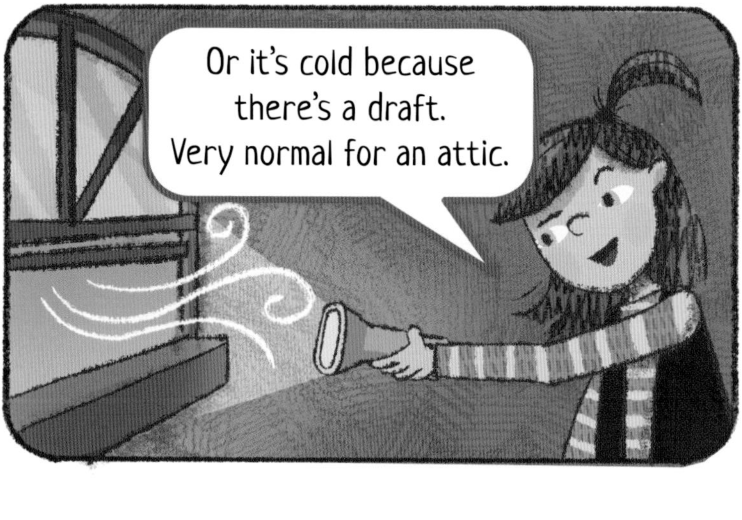
Or it's cold because
there's a draft.
Very normal for an attic.

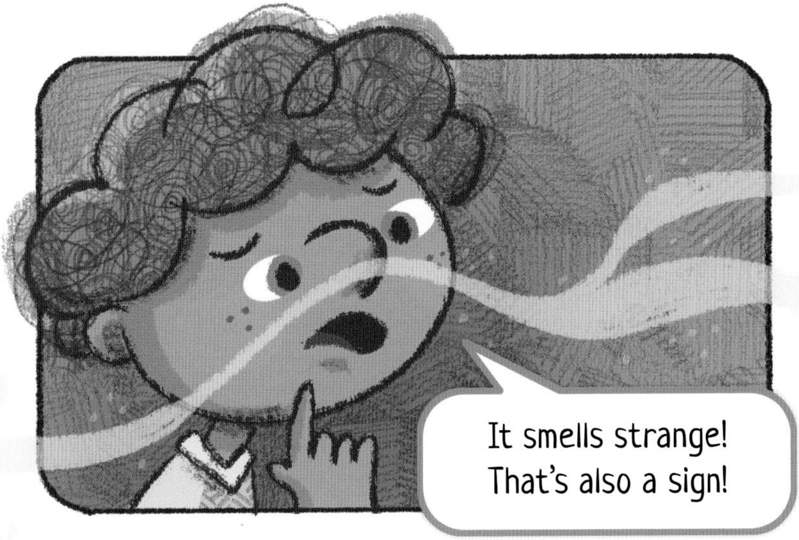
It smells strange! That's also a sign!

It DOES smell strange. But when I point my flashlight at the shelf, I see there is lots of dust.

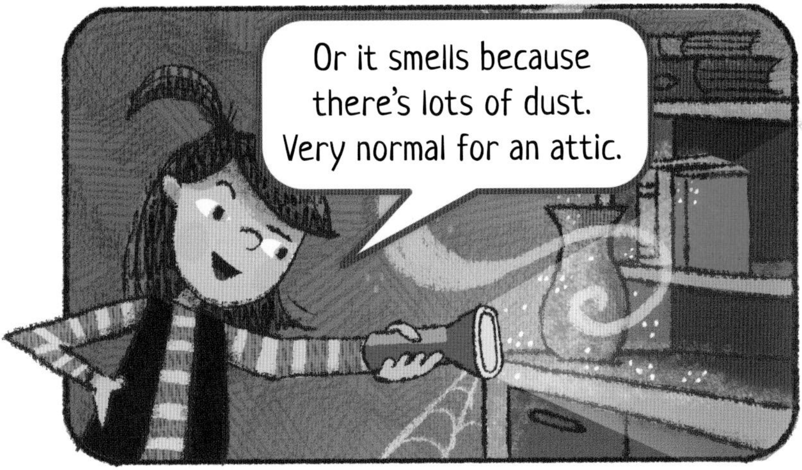
Or it smells because there's lots of dust. Very normal for an attic.

Maybe there isn't any new evidence here after all.

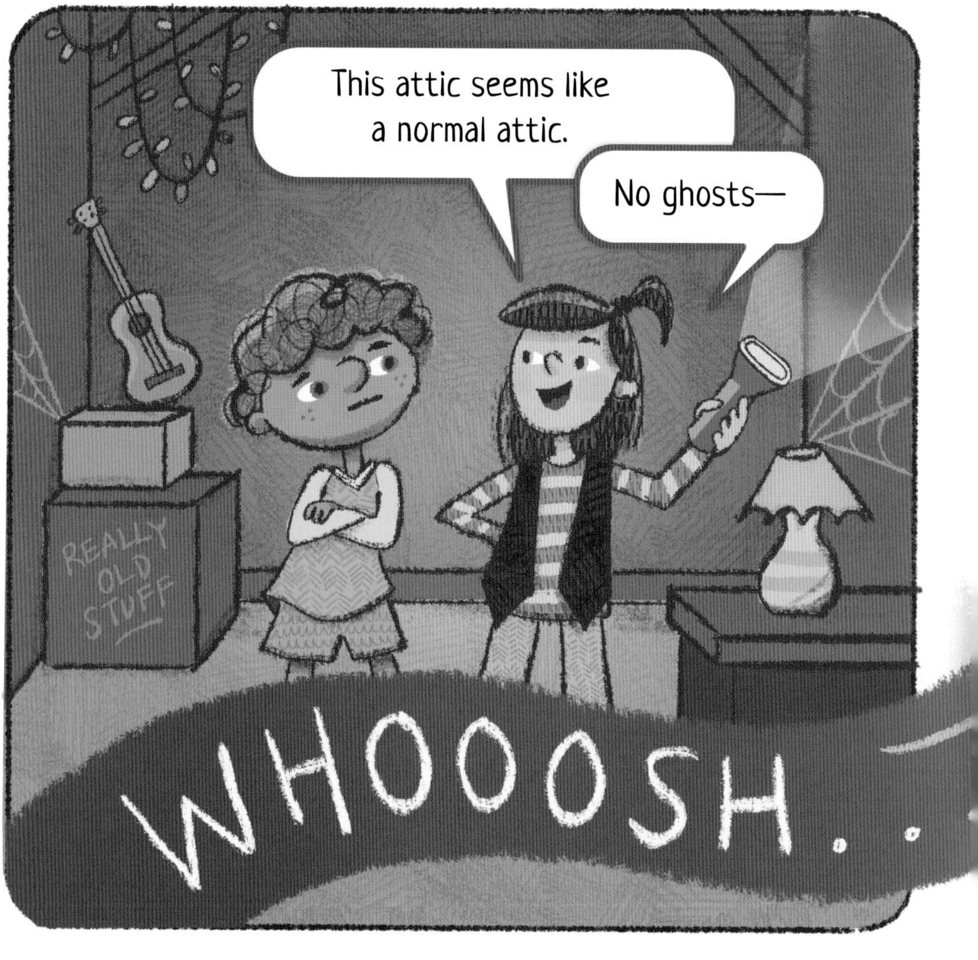
This attic seems like a normal attic.
No ghosts—
REALLY OLD STUFF
WHOOOSH. . .

But wait!

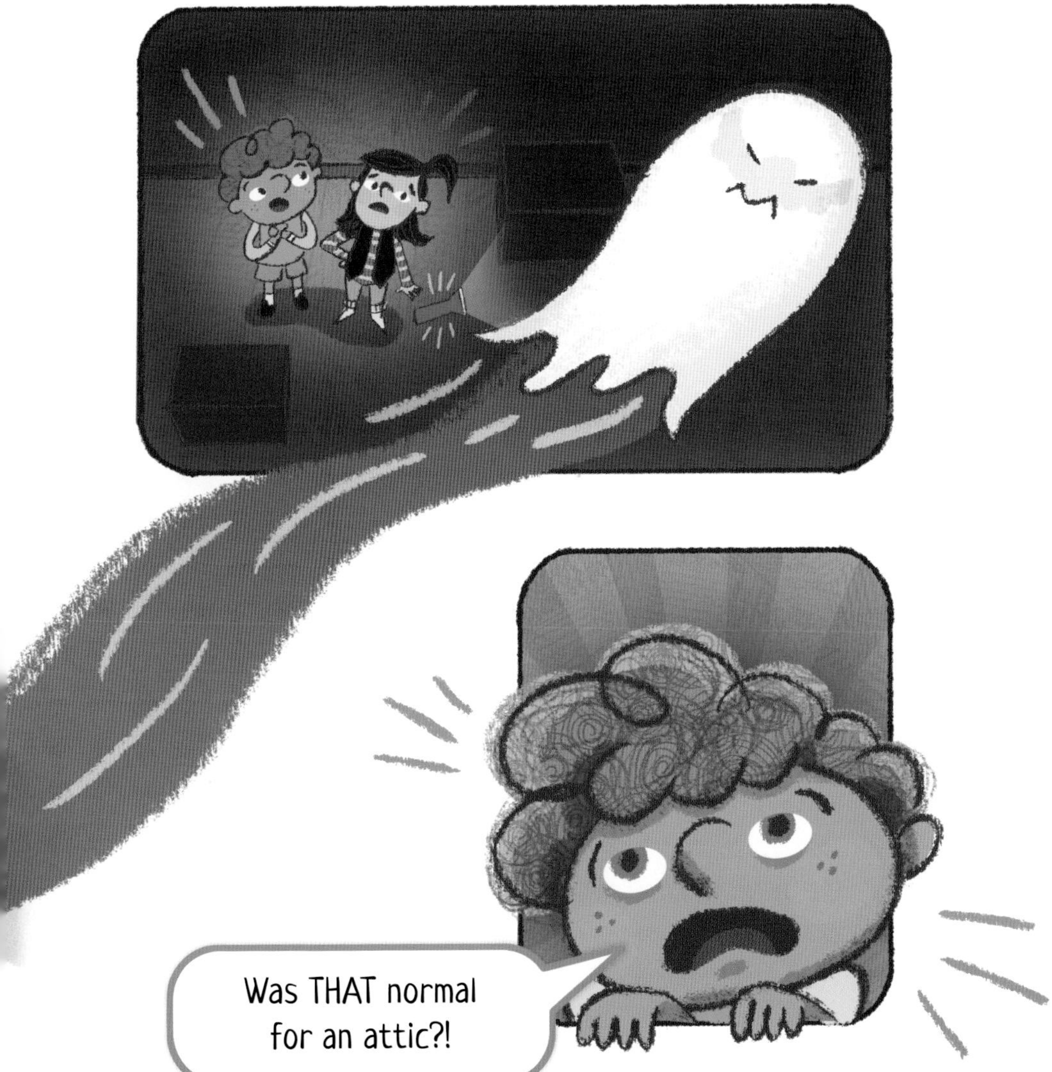
Was THAT normal
for an attic?!

Chapter Nine

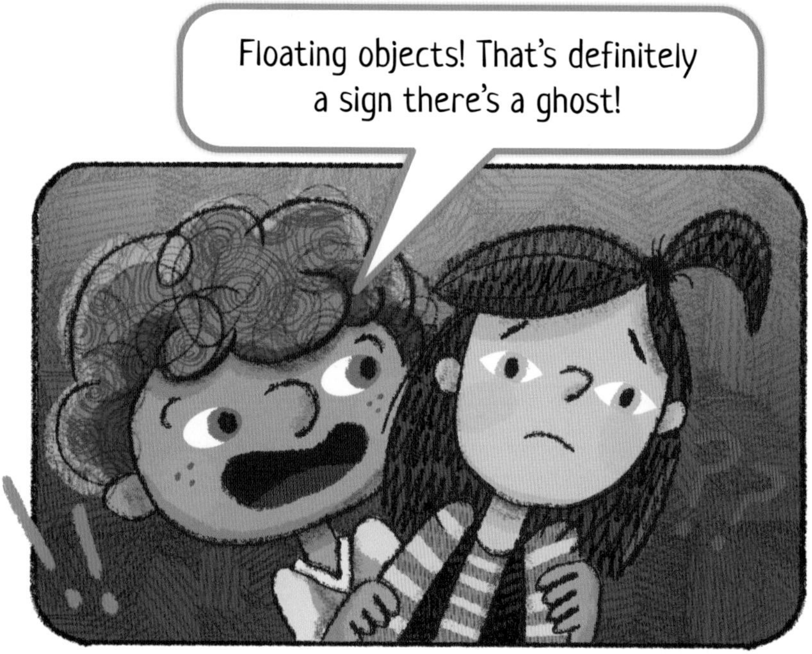
Floating objects! That's definitely a sign there's a ghost!

Once again, more investigation is needed.

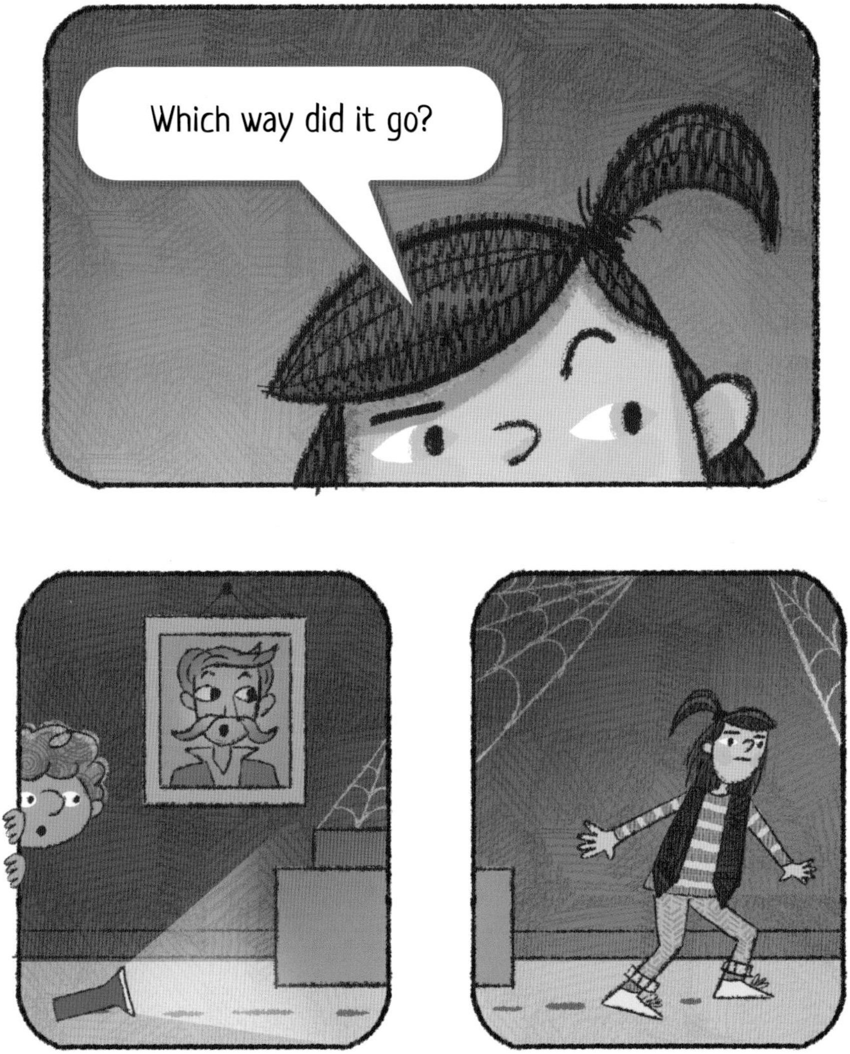
Which way did it go?

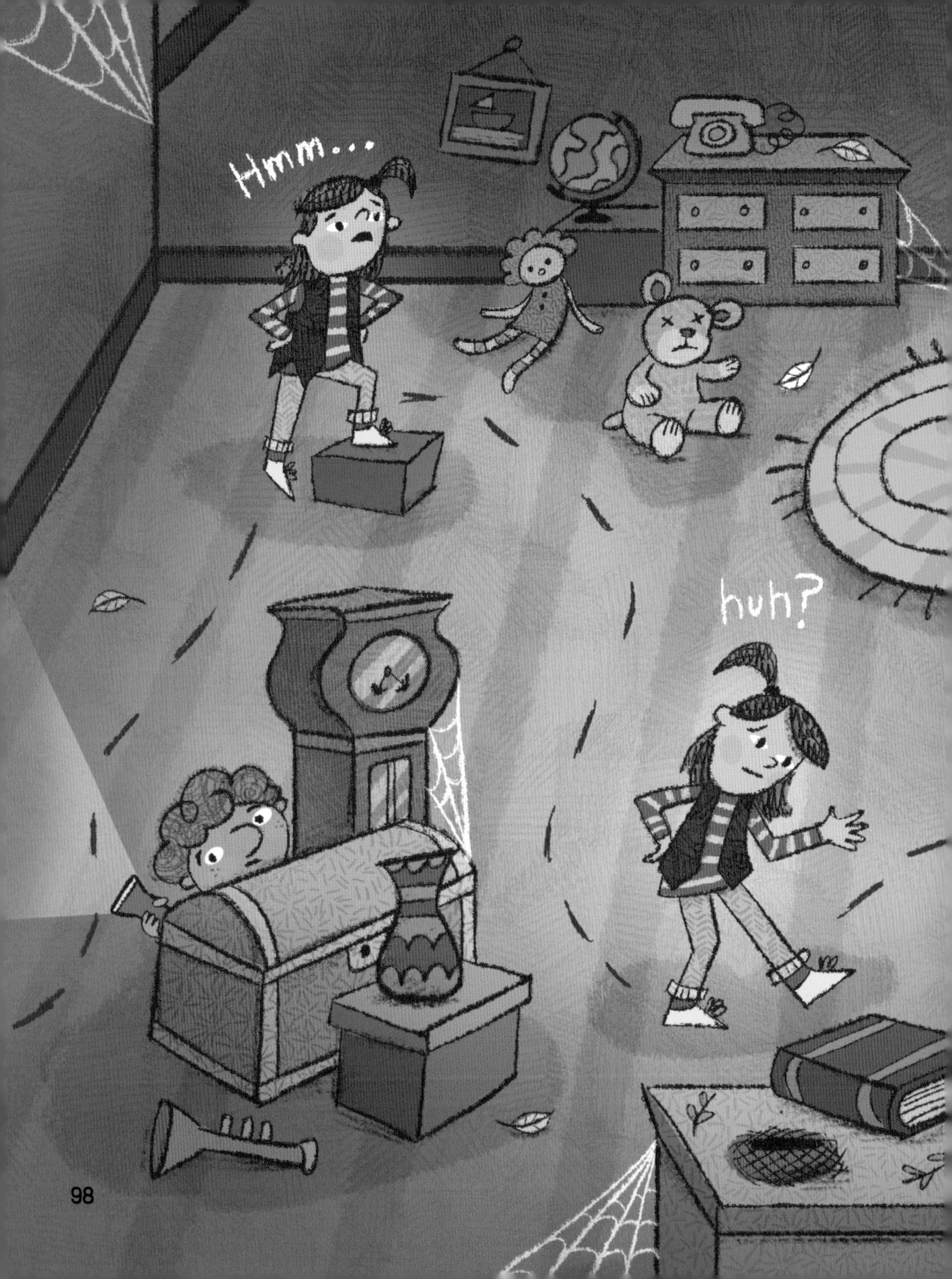
Hmm...
huh?

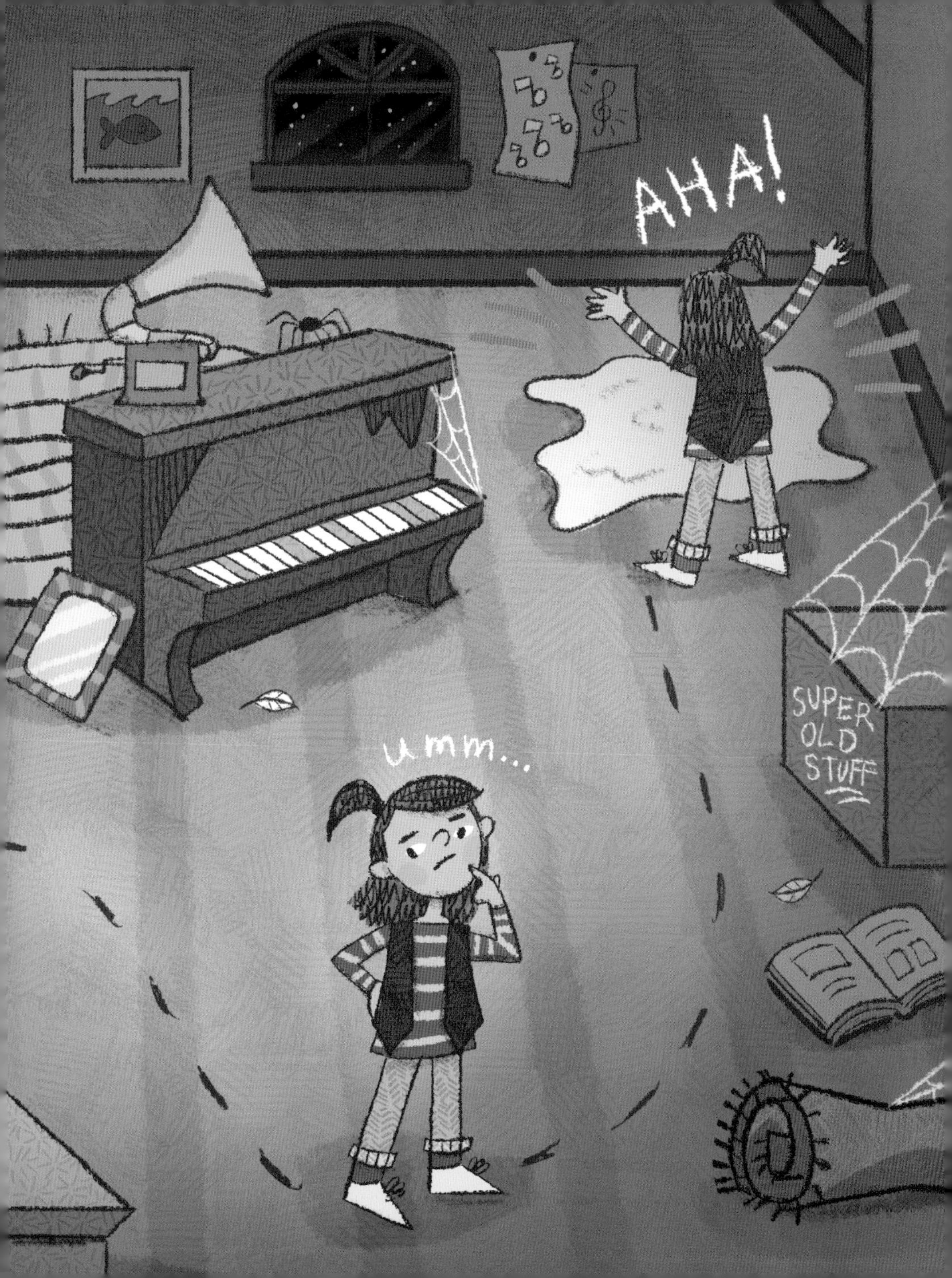
AHA!
SUPER OLD STUFF
umm...

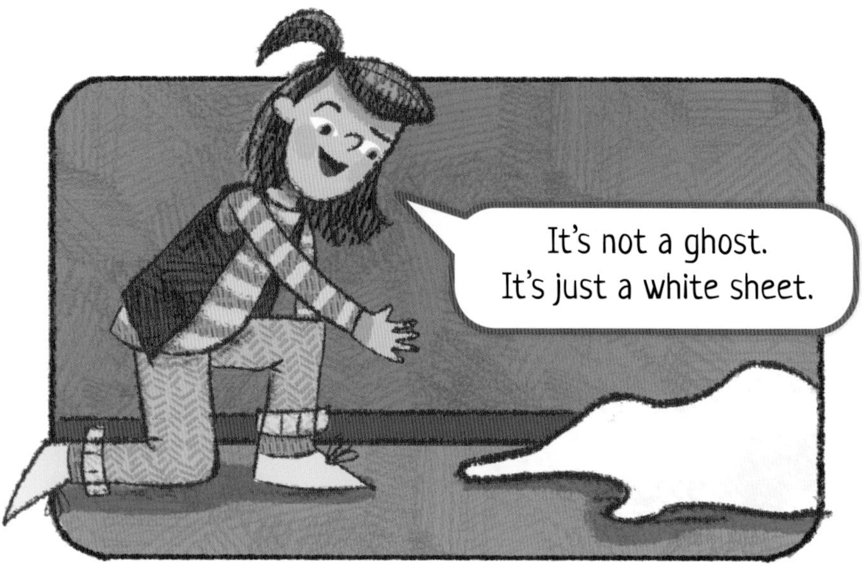
It's not a ghost.
It's just a white sheet.

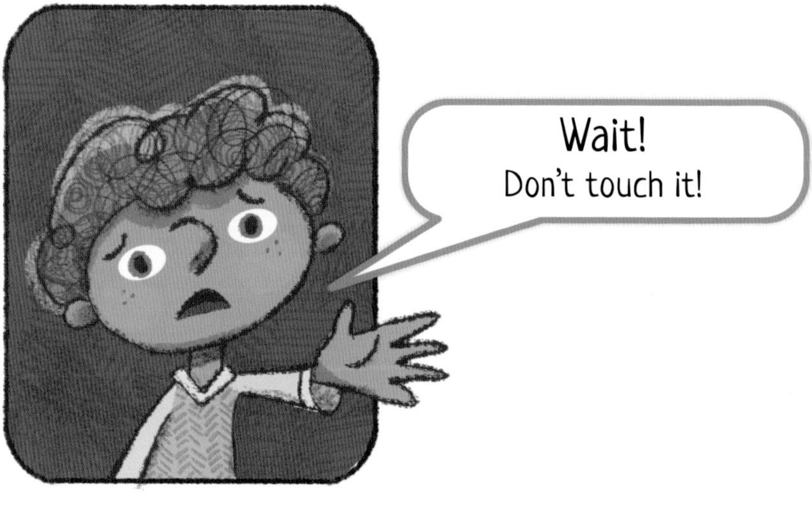
Wait!
Don't touch it!

. . . It's moving!

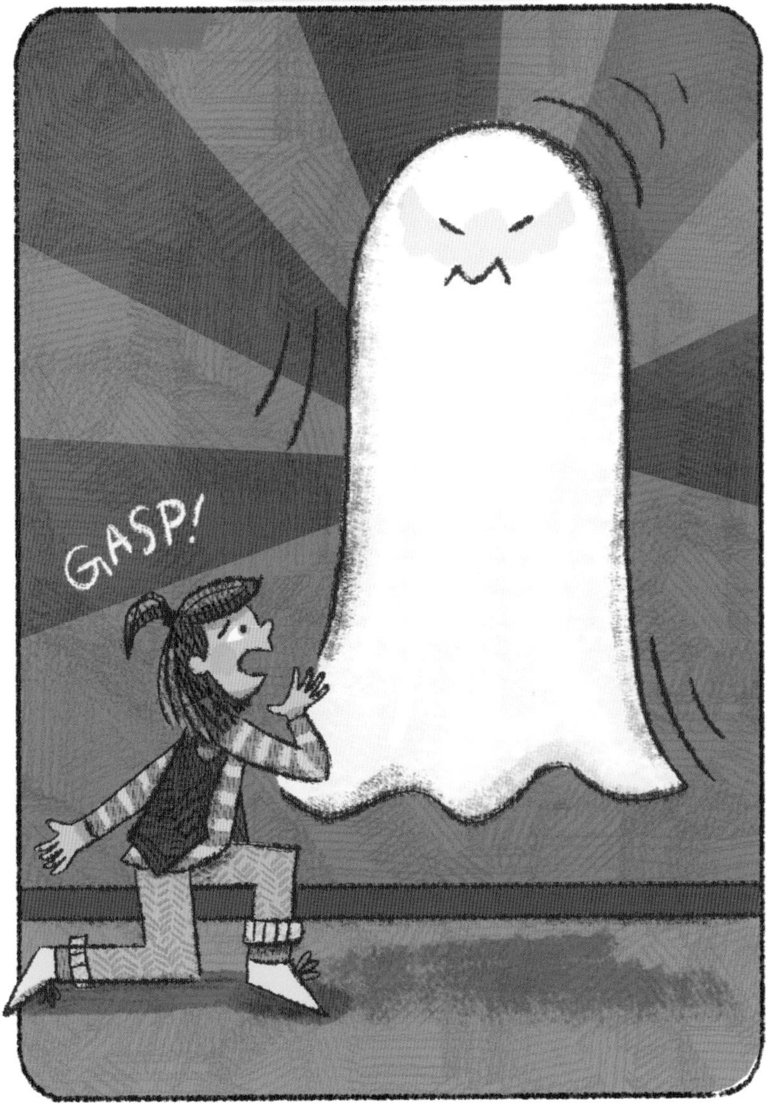
GASP!

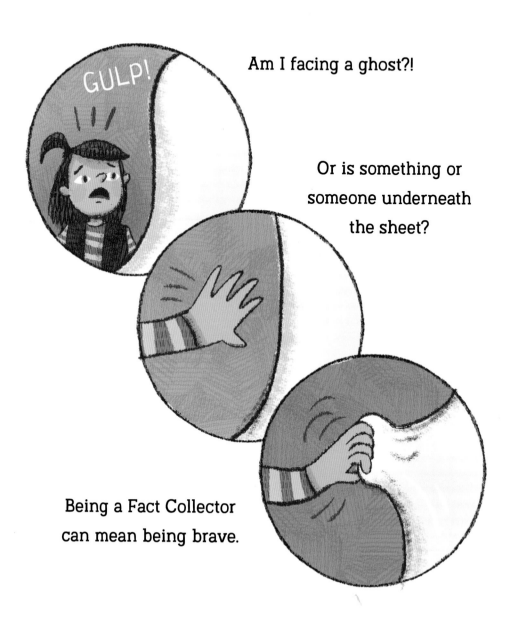

Am I facing a ghost?!

Or is something or someone underneath the sheet?

Being a Fact Collector can mean being brave.

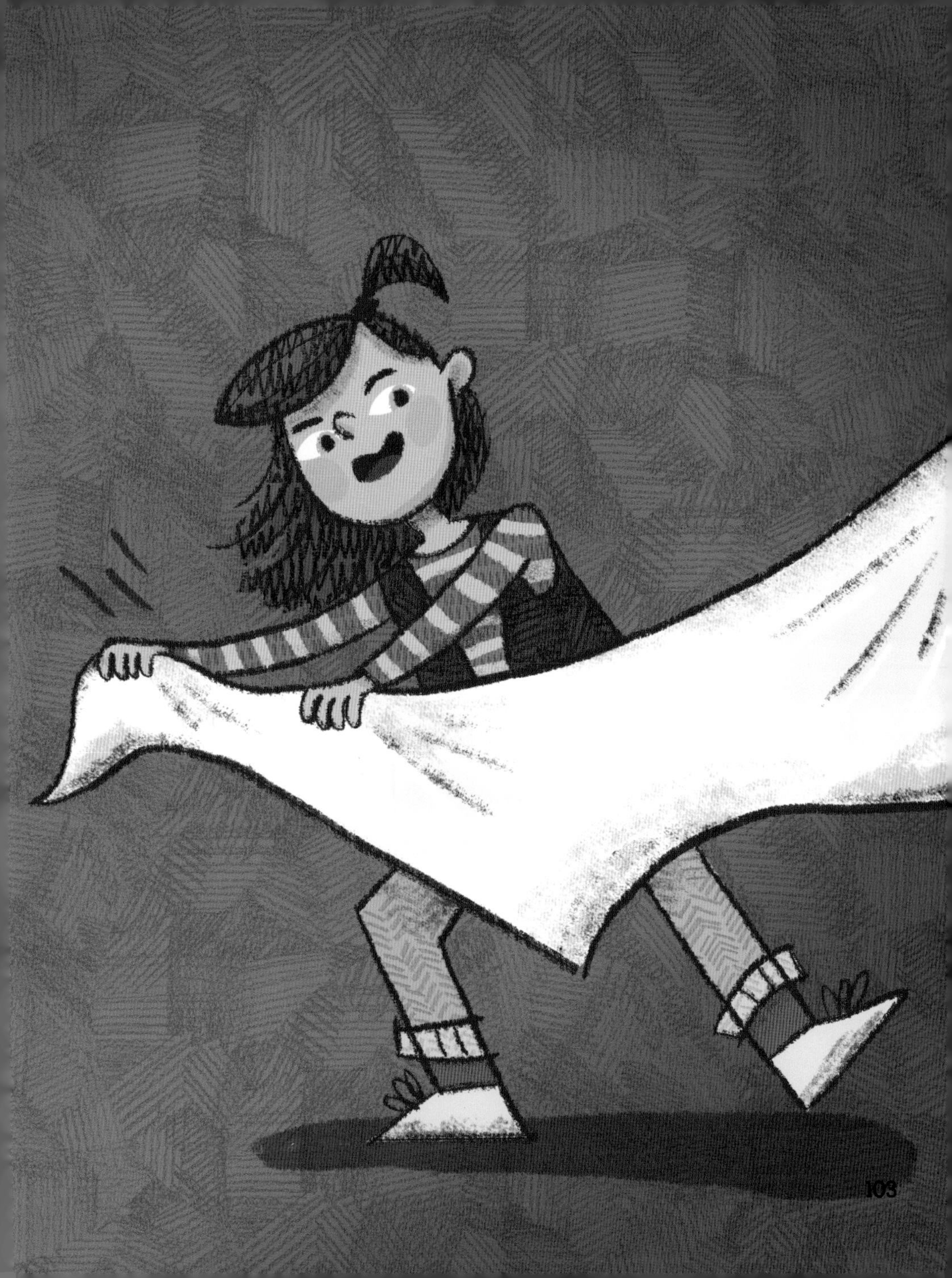

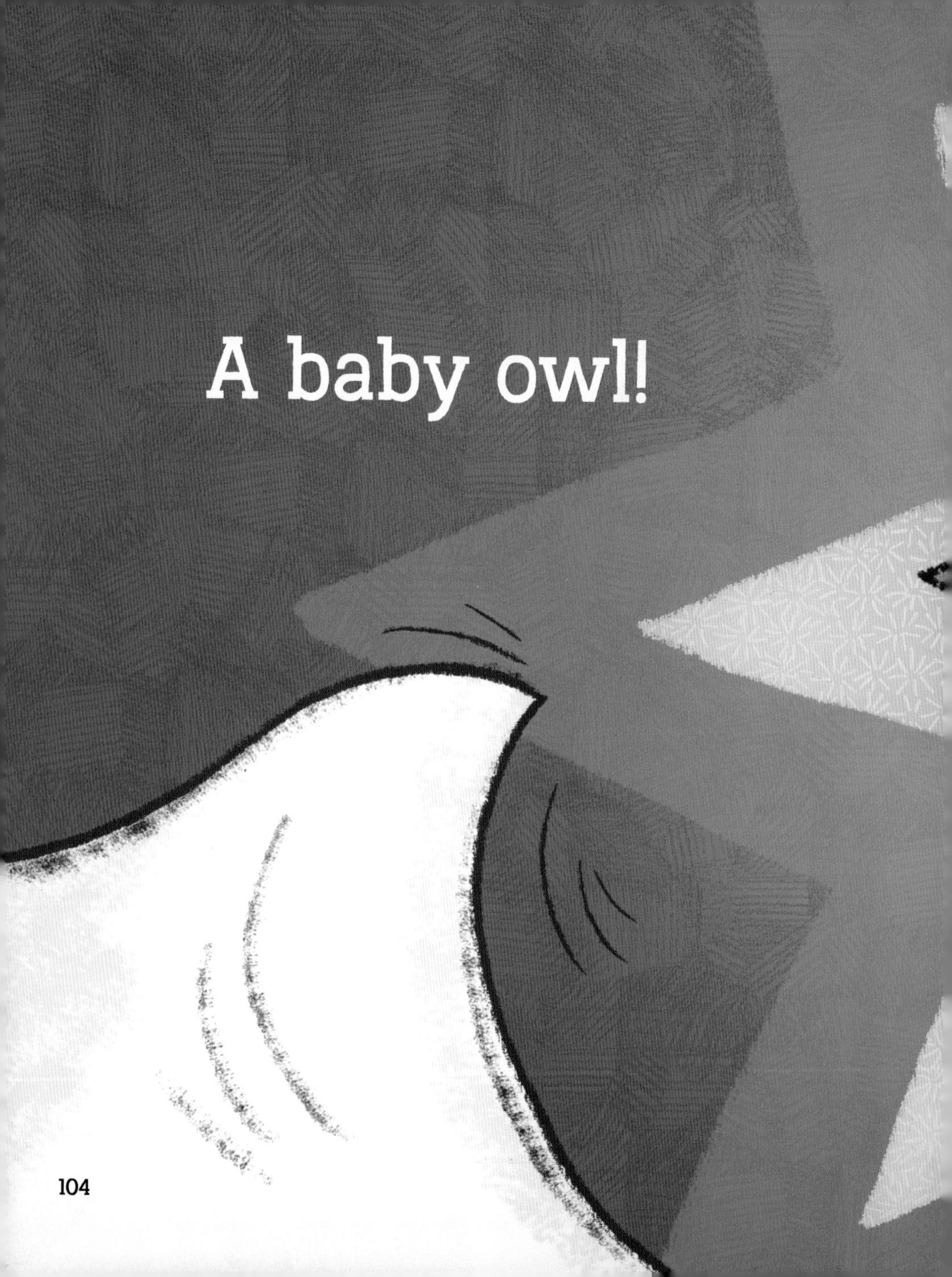

A baby owl!

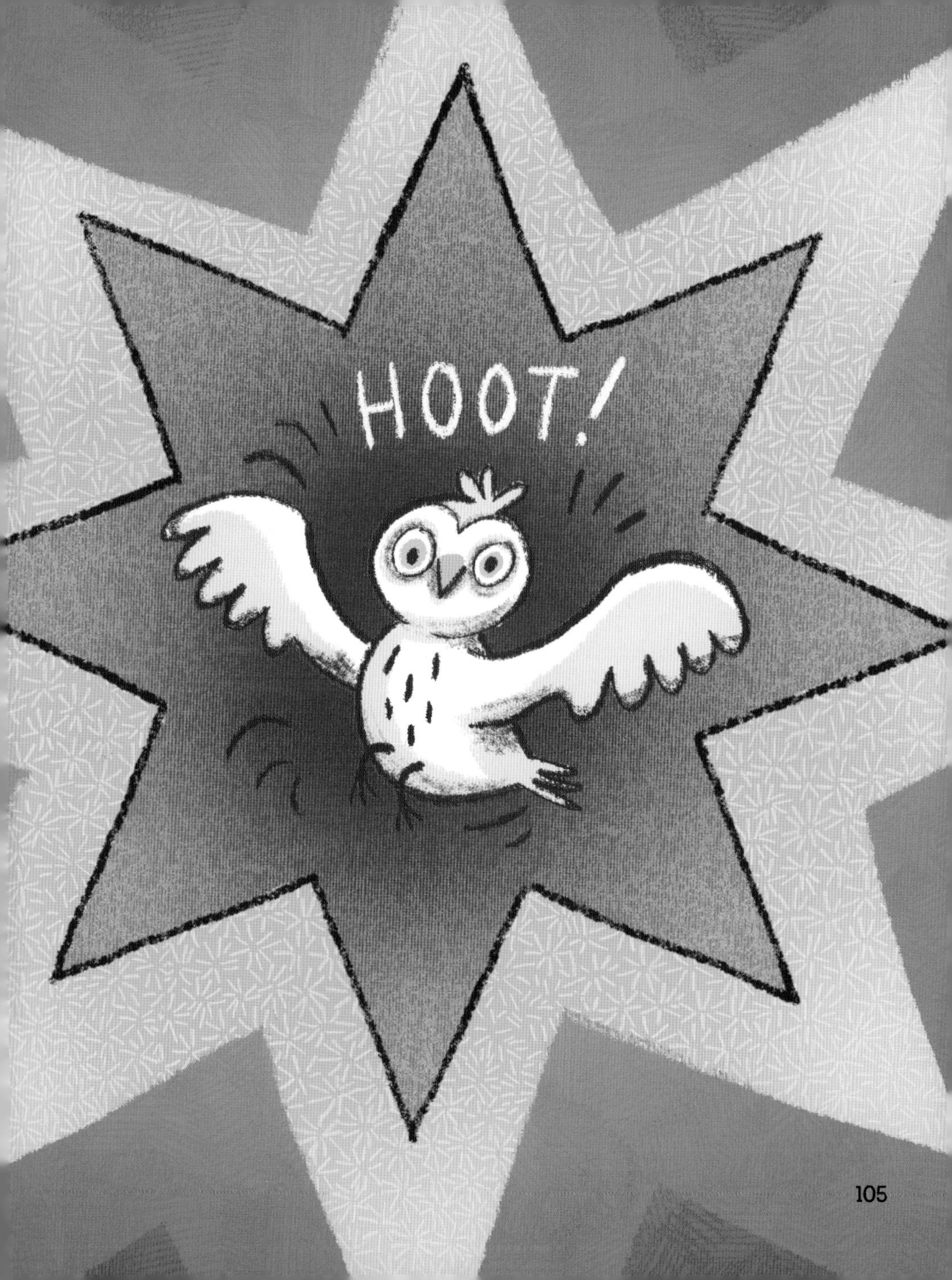
HOOT!

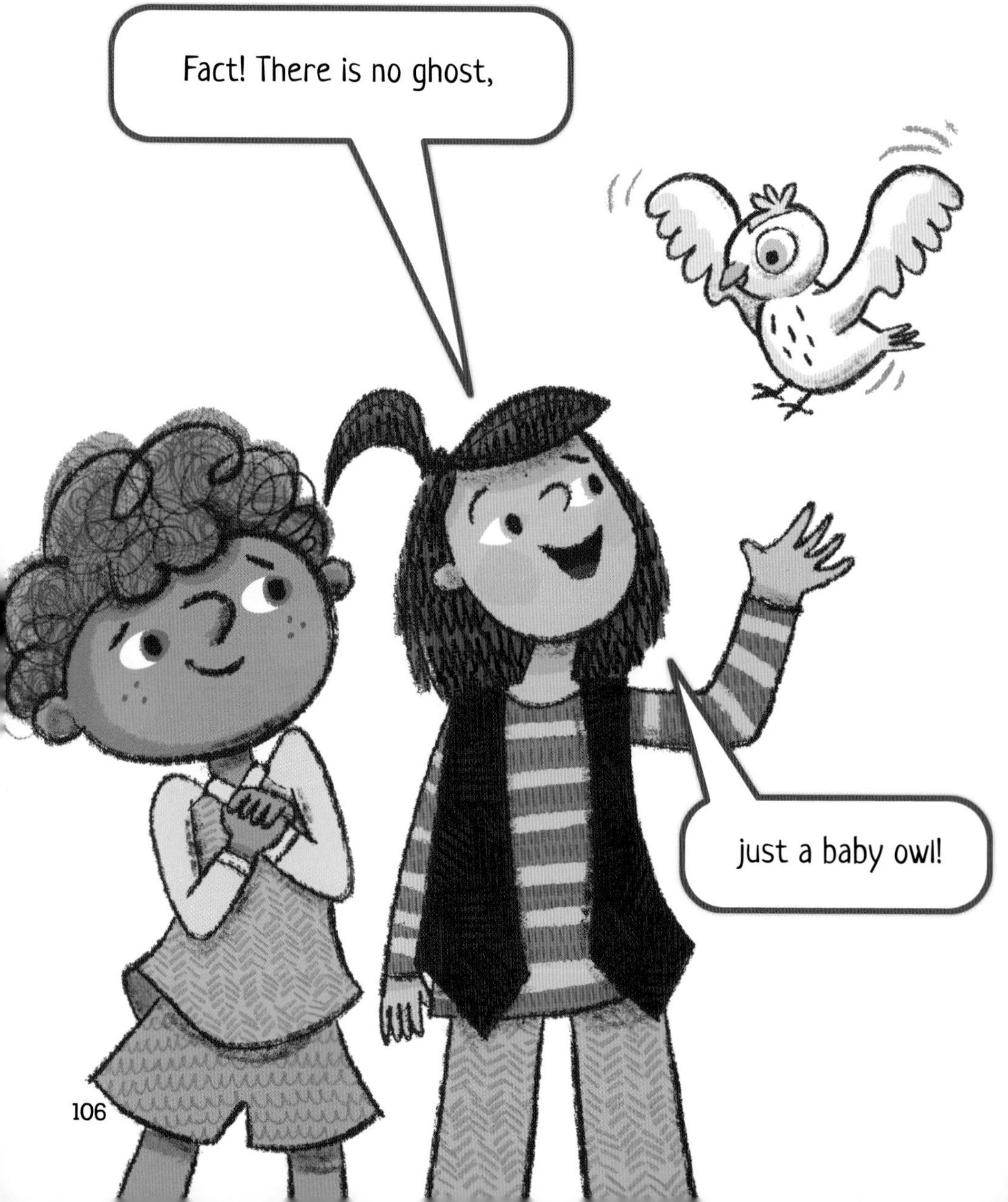
Fact! There is no ghost,
just a baby owl!

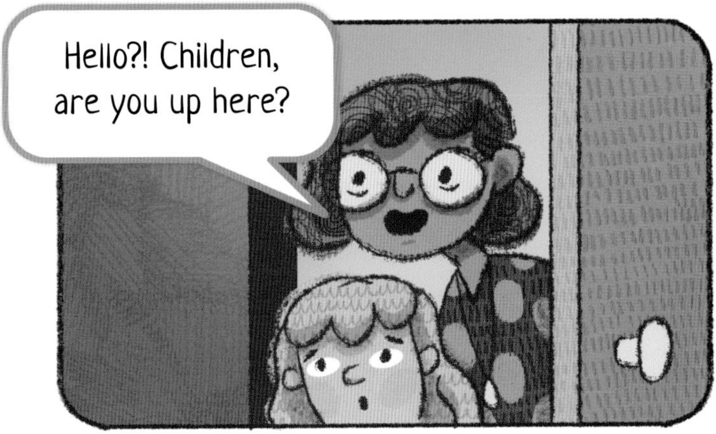
Hello?! Children, are you up here?

It's Karla and her grandma.

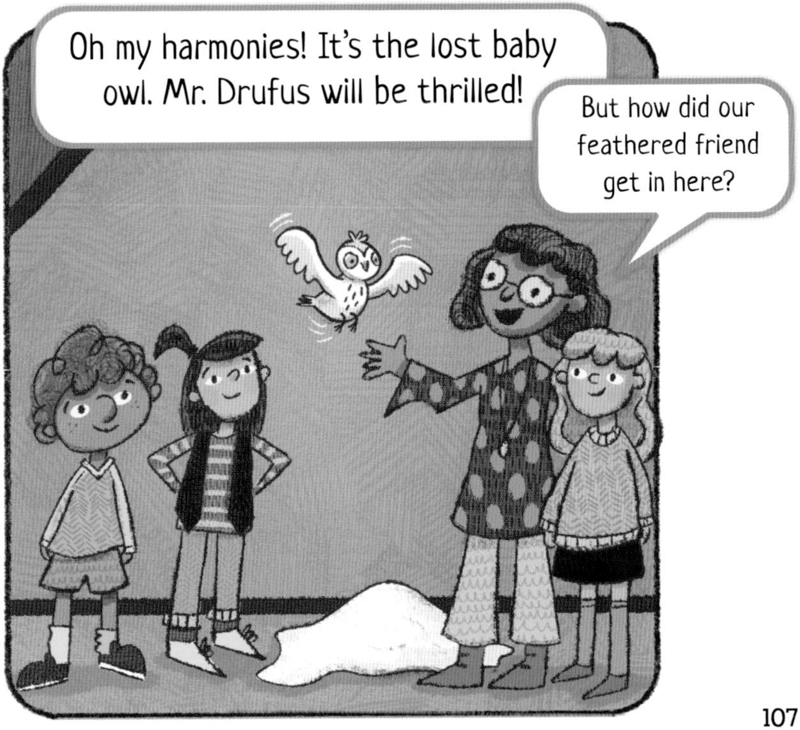
Oh my harmonies! It's the lost baby owl. Mr. Drufus will be thrilled!
But how did our feathered friend get in here?

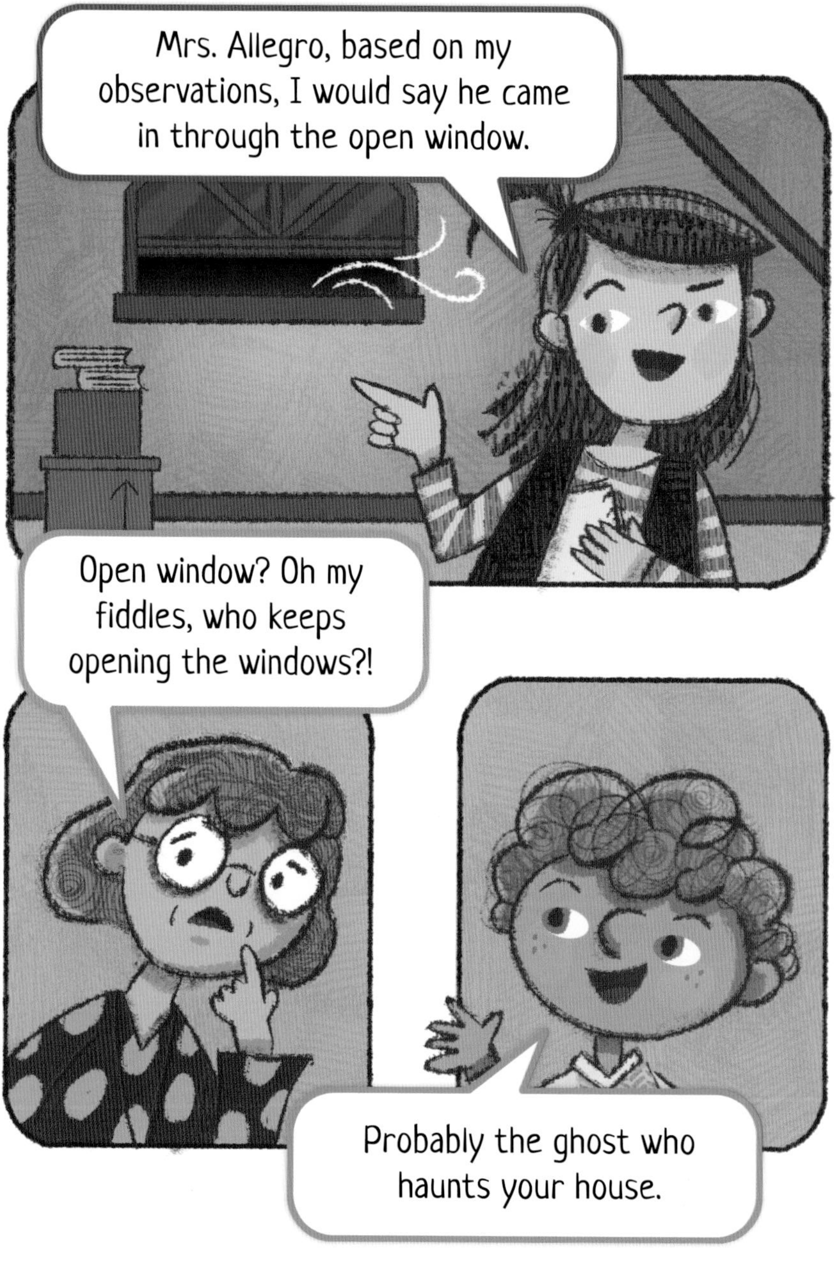
Mrs. Allegro, based on my observations, I would say he came in through the open window.
Open window? Oh my fiddles, who keeps opening the windows?!
Probably the ghost who haunts your house.

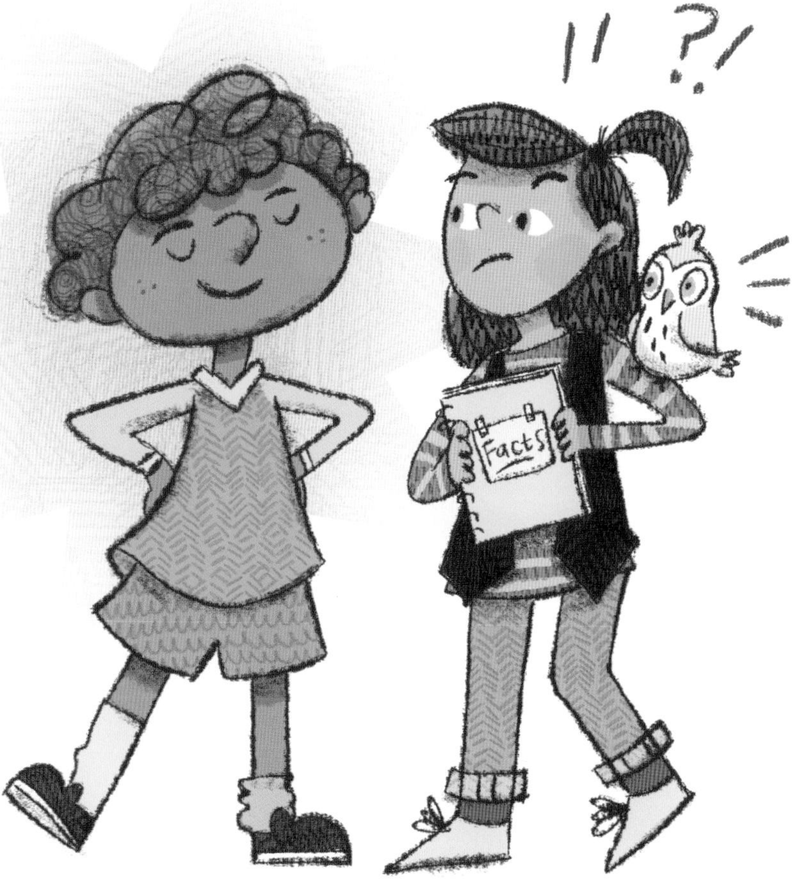
!! ?!
Facts

Even when you have fully investigated, made clear observations, and proven the facts, some people still come to their own conclusions.

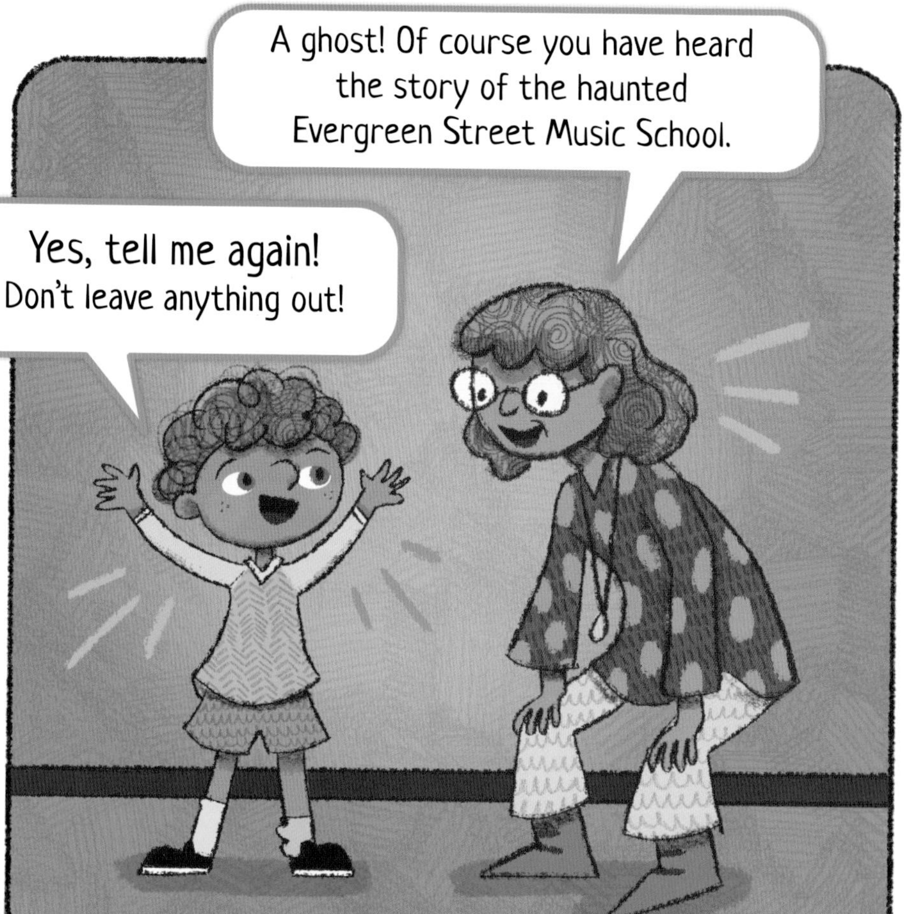
A ghost! Of course you have heard the story of the haunted Evergreen Street Music School.
Yes, tell me again! Don't leave anything out!

111

Hmm . . . But here's a little secret I recently learned.

A good story, either fact or fiction,

brings people together.

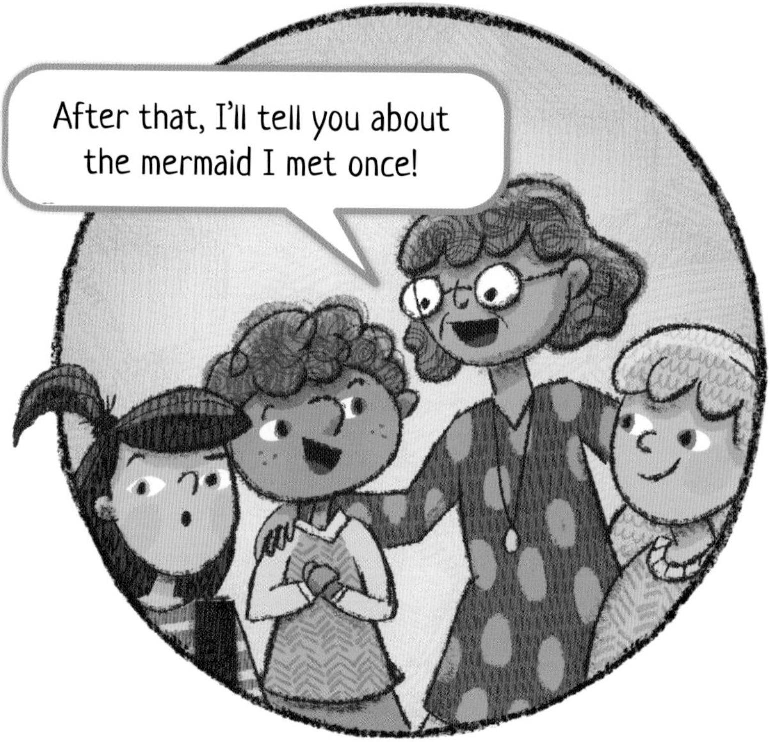
After that, I'll tell you about the mermaid I met once!

Oh dear.